MURDER AT GOOSE RAPIDS

by

Frank Fields

Dales Large Print Books
Long Preston, North Yorkshire,
BD23 4ND, England.

British Library Cataloguing in Publication Data.

Fields, Frank
　　　Murder at Goose Rapids.

　　　A catalogue record of this book is
　　　available from the British Library

　　　ISBN　1-84137-023-1 pbk

First published in Great Britain by Robert Hale Ltd., 1996

Copyright ' 1996 by Frank Fields

Cover illustration ' Prieto by arrangement with Norma Editorial S.A.

The right of Frank Fields to be identified as the author of this work has been asserted by him in accordance with the Copyright, Designs and Patents Act, 1988

Published in Large Print 2000 by arrangement with Robert Hale Ltd.

All Rights reserved. No part of this publication may be reproduced, stored in a retrieval system, or transmitted in any form or by any means, electronic, mechanical, photocopying, recording or otherwise without the prior permission of the Copyright owner.

Dales Large Print is an imprint of Library Magna Books Ltd.

Printed and bound in Great Britain by
T.J. (International) Ltd., Cornwall, PL28 8RW

MURDER AT GOOSE RAPIDS

US Marshal Ellis Stack is called in to the remote cattle town of Goose Rapids to investigate the murder of Sheriff Dan Robbins. The presence of three known outlaws seems to indicate that one of them is responsible, but matters are complicated by a feud between the two largest ranchers and by the fact that Dan Robbins had killed the youngest son of one of them. Before Ellis can answer all the questions and restore law to Goose Rapids he must face a kidnapper and murderer – and all the odds are against him.

ONE

'Do you reckon he'll do it, Pa?'

The question was asked by Adam Gray, the youngest, at seventeen years, of William Gray's five sons as a herd of cattle were driven along the dry river-bed towards the one source of water remaining on the Gray ranch.

'Sam Paxton's capable of doin' anythin',' muttered William Gray in reply. 'He wants this piece of land an' he's made it plain he ain't too fussed just how he gets his hands on it.'

It had been a long, dry, hot summer, the usual spring rains had not materialized and water to nourish the cattle had become a very scarce commodity not only on the Gray ranch but also on the adjoining Paxton ranch. Once, William Gray had been the largest landowner in the territory, but gradually Sam Paxton had acquired the few smaller surrounding ranches and now he had become the biggest landowner. Paxton now had his sights set firmly on the Gray ranch and particularly, since the drought, on the one part of the ranch containing water.

It was not so much that Paxton needed the water, although all ranchers could never get enough, but it just so happened that the one remaining source on the Gray ranch bordered Paxton land.

Thus far William Gray had resisted all offers made by Sam Paxton to buy the land and even he had to admit that the offers had been very fair and it had only been the future of his sons he was thinking about when he refused.

The decision had not been William's alone; all his sons and his one daughter had made it plain that they were very much against getting rid of any land. In fact they had urged their father to buy some of the smaller spreads, but apart from two on the far side of his lands, well away from Paxton, the Grays had been unable to compete with Paxton who had apparently been a very rich man before he arrived in the territory.

Since the last offer had been made and refused some six months earlier, Sam Paxton had become increasingly aggressive both in his manner and his deeds towards all members of the Gray family. There had even been an earlier suggestion that a marriage between William's daughter, Caroline, and one of Paxton's two sons might solve the situation but nothing had come of it since Caroline had never liked either boy and they in turn did not like her since she could hardly be described as the best-looking girl in the territory. At over 200lbs in weight and now aged twenty-five, suitors were not easy to find, and she was not prepared to marry just anyone. As things were, none of the men in the Gray household was all that keen to be rid of her. Since the death of their mother some two years earlier she had assumed the role of cook and washerwoman, a role with which she seemed completely satisfied.

The reason for Adam Gray's question was that Sam Paxton had threatened to drive his own cattle to the water and take it over by force. When it came to force of arms, Sam Paxton could outshoot the Gray family whenever he chose.

Apart from his five sons, William Gray could only muster three other ranch hands, two full-blooded Sioux Indians and one Negro, a runaway slave. Sam Paxton on the other hand could arrange a formidable array of men, including three who were reputed to be nothing more than hired killers with prices on their heads although it seemed that nobody, including Sheriff Dan Robbins from the nearby town of Goose Rapids, could confirm or deny the rumour. Due to the power that Sam Paxton now wielded, there were few who cared all that much, more intent on keeping themselves out of any trouble.

'Best be on our guard,' said Gray senior as the cattle raced towards the water which miraculously appeared in a large bend in the now dry river-bed. 'Adam, you go up there an' keep your eyeballs peeled, although I don't think he'll risk an open range war just yet.' The youngest Gray nodded and obediently urged his horse to climb the steep bank and small hill from where he had a commanding view of the surrounding countryside.

One of the other sons, Pete, climbed the bank on the other side and rode off the half-mile or so it took to reach the boundary of Gray land to inspect the stout wire fence that had been erected. He returned to announce that there was no sign of damage.

Despite his assurance to his sons that he did not believe that Sam Paxton was prepared to risk an open range war, William Gray had the uneasy feeling that Paxton was no longer bluffing. He had recently used force against one small rancher, driving him off his land and, by some legal trickery, produced a bill of sale apparently signed by the rancher. In all this the sheriff, Dan Robbins, had taken no action at all and was strongly suspected of being in Sam Paxton's pay.

Robbins, of course, strenuously denied this, as did Sam Paxton who claimed that the sheriff was in fact in the pay of William Gray. Whatever the rights and wrongs of it, it certainly appeared that Sheriff Dan Robbins was prepared to simply sit back and do nothing.

This stretch of water was vital to the survival of the Gray ranch and, should it fall to Paxton all knew that they might as well just pack up and leave. Sam Paxton was only too well aware of this fact too, which was why he was quite happy to concentrate on this one small piece of land and ignore the remainder.

The pool of water stretched along the river-bed for about 200 yards and the level of water hardly varied even in the worst drought years, fed as it was by an underground stream. However, it was a strange fact that the water would not flow down the river-bed, disappearing underground again at the end of the pool. It was the constant height and flow of water which made the pool so vital. In normal wet years there was sufficient drainage from the land to form small lakes all across the ranch and these normally sufficed to keep the stock watered. It was years such as this, perhaps one in four, when this particular source came into its own.

The cattle were allowed to drink their fill before being driven back along the river-bed to the comparative safety of a very large paddock close to the Gray homestead. There were two other herds and it was now the daily routine to drive one herd to the pool every day. To drive all 5,000 head to the pool at once would have been too difficult and William Gray had learned from experience that water once every three days was just enough to keep the herds fairly healthy.

Normally all the boys and the three hired hands would eat in the house together, but this time the old man insisted that a lookout be posted within sight of the pool and within gunshot hearing distance of the house. Nobody objected and one of the Indian hands took first watch, to be followed by the other Indian four hours later. Adam Gray volunteered to take the third watch from midnight until four in the morning. The instructions to all men were simple: if they saw or heard anything, they were to do nothing except fire one single shot to attract attention at the house.

The chosen lookout was a rocky hill situated on the bank of the river about half a mile from the pool. During daylight hours they would be able to see everything and during darkness there was little chance of not hearing a herd of perhaps 2,000 cows.

The moon was high and bright as Adam Gray relieved the second watch but despite the brightness it was difficult to make out many details and only a thorough knowledge of the land told him what the various shadows were.

It must have been almost two in the morning when Adam heard, quite distinctly, the snort of a horse close by, although plainly somewhere below his lookout point. At first he could see nothing and rather than fire the signal as he had been told, he decided to wait until he did see someone. It was just possible that the snort had come from a wild horse, there were known to be at least three roaming the ranches, horses for some reason abandoned and left to turn wild.

He heard the snort again and this time he saw both horse and rider slowly ambling along the edge of the river. This time Adam did raise his gun and fire...

'Two shots!' exclaimed William Gray, rubbing his eyes as he emerged from his bedroom.

All the others, including his daughter,

Caroline, had tumbled out onto the verandah before him, mostly in their underclothes but all clutching rifles. They stared into the darkness as if expecting something else to happen. When the old man arrived they waited for his instruction.

'Let's go!' he ordered.

There was no attempt at saddling horses, everyone except Caroline simply raced into the darkness in the direction of the lookout which was only about half a mile away. However, they had hardly covered half the distance when a figure on horseback loomed in front of them.

'Tell your boys to hold their fire!' ordered the rider. 'It's me, Dan Robbins!'

'Robbins!' queried William Gray. 'What the hell are you doin' out here this time of night?'

'Right now,' grunted the sheriff, 'bringin' your boy Adam back to you.' He patted something slung across the saddle in front of him. 'There ain't much you can do for him, I'm afraid, he's dead!'

'Dead!' exclaimed Gray senior, an exclamation echoed by the others. 'How? Who killed him? Sam Paxton, it has to be. That does it, this time he's gone too far...'

'Paxton didn't have nothin' to do with it,' interrupted the sheriff. 'I killed him.'

'You!' barked the old man. 'What the hell you wanna do that for, you know Adam never had a lick o'malice in him...'

'How the hell was I to know it was Adam?' grated the sheriff. 'All I knew was someone shot me an' I shot back. Seems he got the worse end of the deal.'

'Shot you?' exclaimed Gray.

'That's what I said,' sighed the sheriff. 'I can prove it too if you'll just let me take him back to your place. My shoulder needs some attention.'

There were mutterings of disbelief, but Sheriff Dan Robbins was escorted back to the house where, after double checking that his son was indeed dead and Caroline had cleaned up the wound in the sheriff's shoulder, an explanation of just why the sheriff was so far away from Goose Rapids at that time of night was demanded.

'I'd say you've got a pretty good idea about that,' responded the sheriff. 'Like you, I heard rumour that Sam Paxton was goin' to make a move against that water-hole of yours. You must've heard somethin' too, why else post a lookout?'

'Sam Paxton is always makin' threats,' muttered Gray, 'ain't nothin' new about that, you ought to know.'

The sheriff winced slightly as Caroline pulled extra hard on the bandage she was applying to the injured shoulder. He gave her a withering look but did not complain. 'This was different, you knew that, just the same as I knew it. Anyhow, I took it seriously enough to decide to ride out here an' take a look.'

'And what did you find?' hissed one of William Gray's other sons.

'I found a young idiot tryin' to kill me, that's what I found,' winced Dan Robbins as Caroline once again pulled hard on the bandage, well aware that she was hurting the sheriff.

'And Sam Paxton?' queried Gray senior.

'Not a sign,' admitted the sheriff. 'I reckon that if they were out there the shootin' probably scared 'em off, for now at least.'

'OK,' sighed the old man, 'I'll buy what you say. Only question I've got is just what would you have done had Paxton and his men been at the water-hole?'

'I'll tell you what he'd've done!' sneered James Gray, the eldest son. 'He'd've just smiled, raised his hat an' wished 'em the best of luck, just like he always does. We all know he's in the pay of Paxton. Hell, he could be in on it too. Maybe he was sent out here to check things out.'

'James,' sighed Dan Robbins, 'this time I'll let it pass on the grounds that you're in shock from havin' your brother killed, but get this straight, all of you, I ain't never been an' never will be in the pay of anybody. I do my job as I see fit an' nobody don't tell me how to do it an' nobody don't get no favours from me, no matter who he is. That includes Sam Paxton, an' it includes you.'

'Bullshit!' grated James. 'All I can say, Sheriff, is from now on you'd better watch your back. Me an' my brothers don't take kindly to havin' our kid brother killed, even by you.'

'An' that goes for me!' hissed Caroline giving one final pull on the bandage.

William Gray sighed and shook his head. 'I ain't so young any more an' maybe my age makes me see things different, but right now, Dan, you ain't exactly the most popular person as far as I'm concerned.'

'That's all I've got to say, Sam,' said the sheriff, picking up his hat and standing up. 'You take so much as one step over that boundary fence towards that water-hole an' I'll throw you in the slammer an' throw away the key.'

'You could always try,' laughed Sam Paxton, raising a glass in mock salute. 'Sure you won't have a Scotch, only the best.'

'No thanks, Sam,' replied the sheriff. 'Just remember what I said. Keep your boys away from the Gray ranch. Right now I'd say they were in a mood to take on anyone.'

'Thanks to you, Dan,' grinned Paxton. 'Maybe I'll just sit back an' wait until you've killed 'em all off for me.'

'Then you'll be waitin' a long time!' grunted the sheriff.

Sam Paxton smiled to himself as he stood by the window and watched Dan Robbins ride away from the ranch. He was still watching and smiling as he heard the door open behind him.

'You heard all that?' he asked, knowing that his eldest son, Jeremiah, was standing behind him.

'I heard,' came the reply. 'Maybe it's about time we acted rather than talked. Talkin' don't get us no water-hole an' no land.'

Sam Paxton turned and seemed a little surprised to see that his son was not alone. 'Heggerty,' he said, 'it would seem that you have convinced my brash son that action is the only way forward.'

Frank Heggerty was a recent addition to the Paxton ranch, employed primarily for his alleged skill with a gun. Sheriff Dan Robbins was in possession of a wanted poster on him and, although he claimed that nobody influenced him in carrying out his duties, he had decided that for the moment at least it was easier to turn a blind eye to the man and two others employed for the same reason.

'You didn't have no complaints about how we persuaded the Smiths to give up their land,' responded Heggerty.

'That's because I never asked,' replied Paxton. 'All I know is I got a piece of paper which says Smith sold that land to me.'

'And that's how it will be with the Grays,' said Jeremiah. 'You just give us the go-ahead an' it'll soon be sorted out.'

'Just like you were going to sort it out last night,' hissed his father. 'All I can say is you ought to be thankin' me for stoppin' it. It's one thing tacklin' somebody like Smith but

William Gray and his sons are a different matter. He has a lot of support in this territory, remember that. He was here first and he almost built Goose Rapids. Sure, last night you could probably have taken over that waterhole and maybe even wiped out the Grays, but that would have been the end of us.'

'OK,' sighed Jeremiah. 'What do you suggest?'

'I'm not suggesting anythin',' said his father, 'but as long as Dan Robbins is still about there ain't nothin' we can do.'

'Then get rid of Robbins!' grinned Heggerty.

Dan Robbins entered the Lone Bull Saloon and stood by the door slowly surveying the room. There was nothing unusual in this, it was a scenario repeated night after night at about this time, when he made his regular evening patrol of the town. The occupants of the saloon completely ignored him as usual, including one particularly morose-looking young man slouched across the counter. Dan Robbins noted the presence of the young man and went over.

'What brings you into town?' he asked. 'Don't normally see you except on Saturday.'

'Free country, so they tell me,' rasped James Gray. 'Since when did I need your permission?'

'Like you say,' responded the sheriff, 'it's a free country. It's just that it's part of my job to notice things that don't usually happen.'

'Like you noticed Adam?' snarled Gray.

'I've already apologized for that,' sighed the sheriff. 'Maybe it was him who should've thought first.'

'Just a kid!' rasped Gray, draining the glass firmly clenched in his hand. 'You hear that, Robbins? He was just a kid, a kid helpin' to protect his father's ranch, doin' the job you should've been doin'.'

'You're drunk,' asserted the sheriff. 'I'll be round again in an hour. I think you'd be better off home.'

'An hour!' snorted Gray. 'Maybe you won't make it back here.'

Dan Robbins ignored the remark and left the saloon to continue his patrol. The other occupants of the room, although making a pretence of minding their own business, had not missed a single word that passed between the two.

Outside the Lone Bull Saloon, Dan Robbins paused as three riders came into town, pulling up alongside him. The first to dismount was Jeremiah Paxton, closely followed by Frank Heggerty and one of the other hired guns, Slim Cairns. Their arrival puzzled the sheriff since, like James Gray, it was very unusual to see them in town on any other evening than a Saturday.

'Goose Rapids is suddenly gettin' real busy,' Robbins observed. 'What brings you into town on a Wednesday?'

'A man gets just as thirsty on a Wednesday as a Saturday,' sneered Heggerty. 'What's it to you?'

'Especially if the boss, is payin',' retorted

the sheriff. 'Anyhow, maybe it's just as well you came in, saves me a ride out to see you' He ignored Jeremiah Paxton and addressed the two hired men. 'I've been thinkin'...'

'Dangerous occupation for a sheriff!' grinned Cairns. Robbins ignored the remark.

'Don't think I don't know who you are,' he continued. 'There's three wanted posters in my office with your two names on them and Jos McKay. So far I've ignored them and I shall continue to ignore them just so long as the three of you are out of my territory within the next twenty-four hours.'

'Are you ordering these men out of town?' interrupted Jeremiah Paxton. 'You can't do that; they've done nothing wrong, they are lawfully employed by my father.'

'I am and they have,' sighed Robbins. 'All three are wanted for robbery and assault. For all I know they could be wanted for murder too, but I'll not chase that up. All I want is them out of this territory within the next twenty-four hours.'

'And if we ain't?' demanded Heggerty squaring up to the sheriff.

'Then I run you in and hand you over to the marshal,' said Robbins.

The threat of being arrested and handed over to the marshal seemed to concern the two men and Robbins suspected that it was the prospect of a marshal becoming involved which worried them most.

'Paxton was right,' said Heggerty, 'You are more trouble than you're worth. Maybe someone should see you don't cause no more problems.'

'Meanin' what?' asked Robbins.

Heggerty did not answer and pushed past the sheriff, closely followed by Slim Cairns. Jeremiah Paxton held back briefly.

'Are you serious, Sheriff?' he asked.

'About them leavin' this territory?' said Robbins. 'Never more serious in my life, it's somethin' I should've done weeks ago. You just see to it that those men are out of here tomorrow, for their own sakes.'

'And for your sake too?' sneered Paxton

pushing the door to the saloon open and joining his two companions.

As Dan Robbins stood on the boardwalk wondering if he had done the right thing or not, two figures came into view from the alley at the side of the saloon.

'Do you think they'll go?' asked one of the figures, a well-dressed elderly man, Tom O'Hara, the mayor of Goose Rapids. The other man was another member of the town council and owner of the hardware store, Desmond Seely.

'You heard?' asked Robbins, a little surprised.

'We heard,' confirmed Des Seely. 'Like you said, it is something you should have done weeks ago. We agree with you that it could have been more trouble to have arrested them, but they could have been told to leave.'

'Well, now they have,' sighed Robbins. 'Now, gentlemen, I have my patrol to finish so I'll bid you good night.' He touched the brim of his hat and clattered off along the boardwalk not giving either man chance to reply.

'I found him just after midnight,' the young deputy sheriff Hal Gibson said to Mayor O'Hara. 'I couldn't be certain he was dead so I called out Doc Freeman. He confirmed the sheriff was dead and we moved his body into the office. Then I came to see you.'

Mayor O'Hara gave the distinct impression of being far more annoyed at being woken at one o'clock in the morning and dragged from his comfortable bed than the fact that the sheriff of Goose Rapids had just been found dead in an alleyway.

'Er ... quite right too,' muttered the mayor, 'although you are the deputy sheriff, you ought to be able to handle this.'

'I guess I can,' replied the young man, 'but I just thought you ought to be informed.'

'Er ... yes ... you did the right thing,' replied the mayor. 'How did he die?'

'That I don't know exactly,' said Gibson. 'Doc Freeman says there ain't no chance of

27

him doin' a post-mortem this time o' night. He'll get on to it first thing in the mornin'.'

'And your opinion?' asked O'Hara.

The young man shuffled uneasily. 'I ain't no doctor, Mr Mayor, I ain't qualified to say.'

'I said I wanted your opinion,' snapped the mayor, sensing that he had an authority over the young deputy that he had never had over Sheriff Dan Robbins.

'Well, sir, purely from what I could see, it looks like he was stabbed in the heart.'

'Stabbed!' mused the mayor. 'Yes, yes, that would make sense. Just as effective as a bullet and a whole lot quieter.'

'Yes, sir,' agreed Gibson. 'Still, there's nothin' anyone can do until the doc confirms the cause of death. Sorry to have disturbed you. I'll get back to the office.'

'No trouble at all,' assured the mayor, suddenly quite liking the idea of having a sheriff he could control. 'Any time, any time at all. Don't be afraid to ask me if you want any help or guidance.'

'I won't,' assured the young deputy. 'Will you be at the post-mortem?'

Mayor O'Hara looked aghast at this suggestion. 'Goodness, no! What would be the point of such a thing?'

'I just thought you might be interested,' replied Gibson. 'I guess it'll be just Doc Freeman and me.'

Doc Freeman took very little time in declaring that the cause of death was indeed, as they had both suspected, a stab wound to the heart with a fairly wide-bladed instrument; most likely, Doc Freeman asserted, a knife commonly used and readily available at both the hardware store and the gunsmith's.

The town council met in emergency session, primarily to confirm the appointment of Harold Gibson as temporary sheriff of Goose Rapids, but were quick to point out that since the position was only of a temporary nature until he was either confirmed in the post or another replacement was found, his salary would not be increased to that of sheriff.

'Jeremiah Paxton or two of the Paxton hired hands, called...' Mayor O'Hara consulted a piece of paper, 'Frank Heggerty and Slim Cairns, one of them must have murdered the sheriff.'

'That's right,' confirmed Des Seely. 'We overheard all three of them threaten Robbins last night.'

'So I hear,' nodded Hal Gibson. 'I also hear that James Gray made some sort of threat in the saloon. There were at least ten other people heard him say that the sheriff might not make it back to the saloon on his rounds.'

'Well I think it was either Frank Heggerty or Slim Cairns,' insisted Seely.

'Quite so,' agreed the mayor. 'So, Gibson, what do you intend to do about it?'

'Me, Mr Mayor?' replied Gibson. 'Nothin' at all. This ain't a case for the likes of me or you, it's a case for the marshal's office.'

'The marshal!' exclaimed the mayor.

'Good God, man, you're the sheriff now, can't you deal with it?'

'No, sir, I don't think I can,' replied the new sheriff. 'In any case, I believe that all such cases, where the death of a lawman is involved, have to be reported to the marshal's office.'

'Only if the killer is unknown,' said the mayor. 'In this case we know that one of three men killed him.'

'Four,' corrected Gibson, 'It could have been James Gray. On the other hand it could have been someone else entirely.'

'Someone else!' both the mayor and Des Seely exclaimed.

'It's possible,' said Gibson, smiling slightly. 'Anyhow, as Sheriff of Goose Rapids, I have made a decision and that is that the marshal's office must be called in. In fact I have already sent a wire to them requesting assistance. In the meantime I intend to ride out to the Paxton ranch and the Gray ranch and inform them of what has happened and instruct them that no man is to leave the territory until after the marshal gives the all clear.'

'I think you should have consulted me first,' muttered the mayor. 'Did you know that Robbins had ordered Heggerty, Cairns and another man called McKay out of town within the next twenty-four hours?'

'He told me when he came back off his first patrol,' said Gibson. 'Which is why I'd better get out there and tell them not to, if they ever intended to. It could be that even if one of them didn't kill him, they might decide it is safer to leave.'

'It was one of them!' asserted the mayor.

TWO

'You've got some explainin' to do,' hissed Sam Paxton as his son, Jeremiah, Frank Heggerty and Slim Cairns entered the room. 'Dan Robbins is dead, stabbed to death, they say.'

'Yeh, we heard that too, Pa,' said Jeremiah, 'but just what has it got to do with us?'

Sam Paxton looked at his son and sneered. 'Just what has it got to do with us!' he mimicked. 'How the hell did I manage to sire a dimwit like you? You and your brother are totally different. He's got an interest in the ranch, he's out workin' while you spend all your time tryin' to avoid it. How does it concern you? I'll tell you how it concerns you. You three were in town last night and I have a reliable witness who says you threatened the sheriff. Not only that but you, Heggerty, came home alone last night, after one in the mornin' and you had a bloodstain on your shirt.'

'That's easy,' grunted Heggerty, 'I stayed with Aggie Bates most of that time, at least from just after eleven till I left her just after one. She can confirm it.'

'Aggie Bates is just about your standard,' sneered Sam Paxton. 'What about the blood?'

'Cut myself on the chest,' replied Heggerty. 'At least Aggie cut me. We was horsin' about an' she took my knife and threatened to cut my balls off. That's when she cut me, look...' He pulled the front of his shirt apart to reveal a bandage which he also pulled to one side revealing a recent livid scar. 'Anyhow, how did you know about my shirt?'

Sam Paxton reached to the floor behind his desk and lifted up a check shirt as though it were something almost untouchable. 'Annie found it on the kitchen fire this mornin',' he said. 'She knows it belonged to you, she marks all your shirts so's she knows whose is whose. You didn't make a very good job of burnin' it.' Part of the shirt was burned but most of it was not. 'So, Aggie Bates cut you did she? Maybe it would have been better for you if she had sliced your balls off, at least you'd've had a good alibi. As it is I'd say you're prime suspect. If you didn't do it, why the hell try to burn your shirt?'

'You ought to know it's almost impossible to get bloodstains out,' replied Heggerty. 'Anyhow, it's my shirt, I got three more, so I can throw one away if I've a mind to.'

'I'll not argue with that,' agreed Sam Paxton. 'But for my money you're as guilty as hell.'

'Well I don't know nothin' about it,' insisted Heggerty. 'It happened just like I said. Sure, we had a bit of a run in with Robbins, I'll not deny that, just as I'll not deny that he ordered us out of town. That's as far as it went though. I swear to you I didn't have nothin' to do with killin' the sheriff.'

Sam Paxton looked at the other two and sneered. 'I don't suppose either of you know anythin' about it either.'

'We were together all night,' replied Cairns. 'I reckon there must have been at least thirty people in the saloon right up till we left just before midnight and all of 'em knew just who we were.'

'Midnight is just about the time Dan

Robbins's body was found,' hissed Paxton. 'Now we both know, Cairns, that you are very handy with a knife...'

'Not this time!' asserted Cairns. 'I ain't so stupid as to go an' kill a sheriff. Why the hell should I?'

'Because my stupid son and Heggerty here seemed to have some bright idea about getting rid of Robbins so that we could then get rid of the Grays.'

'That's madness,' grumbled Cairns. 'I remember a sheriff bein' murdered some other place I was at. They called in the marshal an' he was worse than the sheriff.'

'Exactly!' snorted Sam Paxton. 'Get rid of the sheriff, it would give us a free hand. I seem to remember you, Jeremiah, sayin' somethin' very similar to that. Well I've got news for you, whichever one of you killed him, right now a marshal *is* on his way and do you know just who that marshal is?' They all shook their heads. 'Marshal Ellis Stack, that's who!'

Heggerty and Cairns looked at each other

in alarm. 'We've heard of him,' said Cairns. 'He's a real hard man.'

'A real hard man,' agreed Sam Paxton. His son, Jeremiah seemed not to understand. 'Now you see why I didn't want anythin' to happen to Robbins. I could handle him when I had to, but nobody handles Marshal Ellis Stack.'

'I can't say as I know the name,' said Jeremiah.

'Then your education is sadly lacking,' said Sam Paxton, glancing out of the window. 'It looks like our new sheriff is ahead of the marshal.' He nodded in the direction of the window.

Hal Gibson was riding slowly towards the house, rifle resting on his hip as if prepared for action.

'I reckon we'd best get the hell out of it,' said Heggerty. 'Me, Slim and Jos McKay have all got prices on our heads, nobody ain't never goin' to believe us.'

'They certainly won't if you run,' said Sam Paxton. 'Right now I'd say your safest bet was to ride this out. They've got to have proof and right now I'd say that's one thing they haven't got. You make a run for it and you're as good as admitting you killed him.'

'Then why has Gibson come here?' hissed Heggerty, drawing his gun.

'Put that damned thing away!' ordered Sam Paxton. 'You stay here and keep quiet. I'll go see what he wants.'

Sam Paxton returned a few minutes later, smiling slightly. 'Just like I said, no evidence. He just came to say that you'd better not leave until after the marshal's been.'

Slim Cairns suddenly laughed loudly. 'We stay and we're sure to be arrested by Stack. Remember there's five hundred dollars apiece ridin' on our heads. We stay and end up in jail or we leave and everyone assumes one of us killed Robbins. Either way I don't like the odds very much.'

'You bloody young idiot!' barked William Gray at his son, James. 'What the hell you want to go and do somethin' like that for?

Sure, we're all sore about Robbins killin' Adam, but we all know in our hearts that it was partly his fault. Ever since he was killed you've been like a bear with a sore head. You've been threatenin' to kill Robbins ever since.'

'But I didn't kill him, Pa!' objected James. 'I didn't even have no gun when I went into town last night. I made sure of that, I knew I couldn't trust myself if I did.'

'He wasn't killed with a gun!' grated his father. 'He was knifed, in the chest. Leastways that's what Hal Gibson said. He also said a whole mess of folk in the saloon are ready to swear that you threatened Robbins.'

'I didn't threaten him!' cried James. 'All I did was suggest that he might not make it back on his rounds.'

'Seems like he didn't,' hissed the old man. 'How do you explain the blood on your shirt and pants? As far as I can see what you said was as good as a threat, especially when he didn't make it back.'

James Gray glanced down at the bloodstain on his shirt and shrugged. 'I don't know where that came from. I know I got me a couple of deep cuts on my arm but I don't know how. All I know is I was too damned drunk to know what I was doin' last night.'

'So you could have killed Robbins,' suggested his sister, Caroline, who had been standing alongside her father.

'No!' insisted James. 'I would remember somethin' like that. I can remember leavin' the saloon 'cos I couldn't find my horse at first. When I did find her I fell into the water trough. I reckon that's when I must've cut my arm. Anyhow, I eventually got on board her an' after that I reckon she found her own way back here.'

'She ought to know the way by now,' sneered Caroline, 'it's been at least three times she's had to do it since Adam was killed.'

'I know,' sighed James. 'I guess I took it harder than most of you. Adam an' me ... we was somethin' special. Anyhow, I didn't kill Robbins, I swear I didn't, on Ma's grave I swear I didn't.'

'Then who did?' asked his father, mellowing slightly.

James thought for a moment and then smiled. 'Jeremiah Paxton. If not him then one of the two hired gunmen he came in the saloon with. Yeh, that's it! I was drunk I know, but not that drunk, not then. The one they call Frank Heggerty left just after eleven and the other two just before midnight. I'm sure of that.'

'And Dan Robbins was murdered at about midnight,' mused the old man. 'Could be, and I do hear Heggerty and the other two have prices on their heads. It has to be one of them, but I don't see Jeremiah havin' the guts to do somethin' like that.'

'Me neither,' agreed Caroline. 'He don't have no guts for nothin'. All he's interested in is gamblin' and drinkin'. Even his pa thinks he's a waste of time.'

'Maybe so,' said the old man, 'but Jeremiah Paxton is a dangerous waste of time.'

'Does Hal Gibson know they were in town last night?' asked James. 'I know I was there but I wasn't takin' all that much notice.'

'I'll bet he does by now,' sighed William Gray.

'Maybe someone should make sure,' suggested Caroline.

Ellis Stack, United States Marshal, had heard of Goose Rapids although he had never had cause to visit the town, even though since becoming a marshal he had tried to make a point of visiting every town in his territory. Goose Rapids however, was one of those as yet still on his list to be visited.

The wire he had received from the new sheriff of the town had been short and business-like, but had contained the essential details. Often such a request would have to fall in line with a series of other requests even though the apparent murder of a sheriff was involved, but there was something about the message which made

Ellis sense that all was not quite as straightforward as it might have been. Besides, he quite enjoyed investigating such cases. It made a change from the usual routine.

He had sent a message ahead confirming his arrival and, as expected, it seemed that almost the entire population of the territory were there, not exactly to welcome but to stand and stare as if a marshal was a strange creature only normally found in some far-off corner of the world.

Ellis could hear mothers threatening erring offspring with the wrath of the marshal if they did not behave themselves. Some boys, fancying themselves as gunfighters, practised their draw with wooden guns or even, in at least one instance, what looked like real guns.

The reception he received was something that he had never experienced before. Sometimes he had to make his arrival and himself known to the local sheriff, but on this occasion all that was missing was a band.

'Welcome to Goose Rapids,' beamed a well-dressed man. 'Marshal Ellis Stack, I take it?' Ellis nodded, almost bemused. 'I am Thomas O'Hara, Mayor of Goose Rapids.' He swung his arm around at a group of other people around him. 'These are fellow members of the council...'

'Nice to meet you,' said Ellis, not caring for the reception. 'First thing I want is a good wash and then a good meal, I've ridden a long way.'

'Of course, of course,' said the mayor, plainly crestfallen at what he saw as a rebuff. 'A room is awaiting you at the hotel across the street...'

'Good!' grunted Ellis, turning his horse in the direction of the hotel. 'Give me an hour and then send your sheriff over.'

'Er ... of course,' replied Tom O'Hara. 'I thought that perhaps you might like to be acquainted with the details...'

'Sheriff Gibson can fill me in,' said Ellis. 'If there's anythin' I want to know from you or the council, I'll ask.'

The entire reception committee appeared very embarrassed as the marshal dismounted his horse outside the hotel, took various things out of the saddle-bags and his rifle and went inside.

'Come in!' called Ellis in response to a knock on the door of his room. A young man entered wearing the badge of office of a town sheriff. 'Gibson?' said Ellis, more as a statement than a question.

'Harold Gibson,' replied the sheriff. 'Most folk call me Hal.'

Ellis looked at the young man and smiled, remembering the time he first started out on his career. 'Just about the same age I was when I became a sheriff,' he said. 'I took over in Red Rock.'

'I know,' said Gibson. 'I reckon most deputies know how you started; you're sort of a figure we all look up to and hope to be like one day.'

'I'm flattered,' grinned Ellis. 'Did you also hear that I spent some time in prison?'

'For something you didn't do,' nodded Gibson. 'Sure, I knew that too. Welcome to Goose Rapids, Mr Stack.'

'Please. Ellis.'

'No, sir,' insisted Gibson, 'it wouldn't be right for the likes of me, especially at my age, to be callin' you by your given name. Mr Stack will do me fine.'

'You make me feel like an old man,' smiled Ellis. 'I can't be more than maybe ten years older'n you.'

'It ain't a matter of age,' smiled the young sheriff. 'Maybe one day, when I've got some experience behind me, it might be right to call you by your given name, but until then I'd be much happier callin' you Mr Stack.'

Ellis felt that this young sheriff was being perfectly sincere in what he said and he did not argue. 'I've had me some reception committees in my time,' he smiled, 'but that one just about beat the lot. Is it always like that?'

'Took me by surprise too,' laughed Gibson. 'I decided to keep out of it. Mayor

O'Hara ain't normally like that, can't think what got into him.'

'A desire to impress or to hide something,' grinned Ellis. 'Which do you think it was?'

Hal Gibson looked at his senior almost in awe. 'It ain't like O'Hara to want to impress anyone,' he said. 'As for wantin' to hide somethin' ... I never really thought about that, but just maybe...'

'I thought as much,' smiled Ellis. 'I seem to have this instinct of knowing when someone is trying to cover something up. Now just what could Mayor Thomas O'Hara be wanting to hide?'

Hal Gibson laughed. 'Mr Stack, sir, I can see just why you've got the reputation you have. Less than two hours in town and already knowin' that our mayor, that perfect pillar of the community has a dark secret.'

'Who said anything about secrets?' asked Ellis. 'Can it really be a secret if the whole town knows about it?'

'Not the whole town, Mr Stack,' replied Gibson. 'I reckon I am the only one to know.'

'And can what you know have any bearing on what happened to Sheriff Dan Robbins?'

For the first time the young sheriff looked uncomfortable. He shuffled a little uneasily and walked to the window. 'I don't know if it means anythin' or not. Maybe it doesn't, in fact I don't think it does, so maybe I'd better keep my mouth shut.'

'I can't force you,' said Ellis, 'and I admire loyalty, but I'll probably find out sooner or later.'

'Not if you discover who murdered Mr Robbins first,' pointed out the young sheriff.

'Which is something I shall do all the sooner if I start by eliminating people,' said Ellis.

Hal Gibson studied the face of the marshal for a moment and then looked out of the window again. 'It ain't so much Mr O'Hara I'm concerned about,' he said, 'it concerns a lady.'

'Ah!' sighed Ellis. 'Isn't there almost always a lady involved somewhere? Purely at a guess I'd say the lady concerned was either Mrs Robbins, widow of the sheriff, or the wife of Mayor O'Hara.'

Hal Gibson did not turn, but continued looking out of the window, remaining silent for a few moments, which convinced Ellis that he was right about the identities of the ladies or lady.

'There ain't no Mrs Robbins,' Hal said eventually. 'She died more'n two years ago.'

'Then the lady in question must be Mrs O'Hara,' said Ellis.

The young man turned, sighed heavily and nodded. 'I know that Mrs O'Hara and Dan Robbins were ... well, you know ... seein' each other, fairly regular like.'

'You know; does Mr O'Hara know and does anyone else?'

'I don't think so,' said Hal, now resigned to the fact that he had somehow been forced to divulge a confidence. 'I don't think anyone else knows, that is. I can't be sure about Mr O'Hara, but I've lived in this town all my life, born an' bred here an' I know everyone and everyone knows me. Believe me there ain't nothin' goes on in Goose Rapids that I don't get to hear about and if anyone had known about Mr Robbins and Mrs O'Hara it would have been too hot to keep to themselves, but I ain't never heard any suggestion.'

Ellis nodded, well aware that it would be impossible to keep such knowledge secret in almost any town. 'How long have you known?'

'Over a year,' replied Hal. 'It bothered me at first, me bein' a God-fearin' man an' all that. I go to church regular and serve as a sidesman. I thought about tellin' the minister about it but, even though I say so myself, the Reverend Chandler is just about the biggest gossip of them all. In the end I decided that it really was no business of mine and forgot all about it.'

'A very wise decision if I may say so,' nodded Ellis. 'Now, Hal, may I call you Hal?' The young man nodded. 'Now, Hal,' continued Ellis, 'sit yourself down and tell me exactly what you know about all this.'

Hal Gibson pulled a high-backed chair from behind the door, straddled it and rested his arms across the back. He told Ellis everything he knew and all about the bad blood between the Paxtons and the Grays. He told him about possible suspects on both sides being in town that night, emphasizing that it was most unusual to see any of them in town on a Wednesday. When he had finished his story, he looked at the marshal as if somehow expecting everything to be instantly clear and that he would announce the name of the murderer without hesitation. He was slightly disappointed when this did not happen.

'So,' said Ellis, who had been lounging on the bed whilst Hal had been talking, 'it would appear that we have four, possibly six suspects...'

'Six!' exclaimed Hal. 'Where'd you get the other two from?'

'Jeremiah Paxton, Frank Heggerty, Slim Cairns and James Gray are the obvious ones,' admitted Ellis. 'But by your own account there are two more. The mayor, Mr Thomas O'Hara, because the sheriff was apparently having an affair with his wife and, remote though it may be, it is just possible that Mrs O'Hara killed her lover.'

'Mrs O'Hara!' Hal Gibson was clearly horrified at the suggestion. 'She couldn't hurt nobody, she's a woman, a God-fearin' woman at that...'

'But not so God-fearing as not to have an affair with another man, and her a married woman,' reminded Ellis. 'I agree, it's probably most unlikely, but it could be that she wanted to end the affair with Dan Robbins but he wouldn't so she saw murdering him as the only way out.'

Hal digested the possibility for a few moments and then shook his head. 'Put like that I guess it's possible, but I can't go along with it, not Mrs O'Hara.'

'As I said, it is most unlikely,' agreed Ellis. 'On the other hand a knife, in my experience, is the second most favourite way for a woman to commit murder. Mind you, that's mostly from what I've heard, I've only ever had to deal with one woman who murdered her husband and that was because he was beatin' the hell out of her and her children.'

'We had one like that a couple of years ago,' nodded Hal, 'just before I became deputy. They weren't from these parts though, incomers from back East. Anyhow, if usin' a knife is the second most popular, what's the first?'

'Poison,' said Ellis. 'That's always the favourite. There's a hell of a lot of poisons about, most growin' wild and they're nearly all impossible to trace. I'll bet my career on there bein' more men killed by poison than by any other method by their wives.'

'Remind me not to get married!' said Hal. 'OK, you've convinced me. Now we have six suspects.'

'At least,' nodded Ellis. 'It is of course possible that it was none of them. You say there's almost nothing that happens in

Goose Rapids that you don't get to hear about, did anyone else have reason to hate or even just have a grudge against Dan Robbins?'

Hal Gibson thought for a minute, rubbing his chin thoughtfully up and down his arm on the chair back. 'No, not that comes to mind. Mr Robbins was a good man, always very fair in the way he treated folk. Sure, there were a few who spent the odd night or even week in jail, but they never seemed to hold it against him. What you will hear is that Mr Robbins was in the pay of either Sam Paxton or William Gray, dependin' on who you're talkin' to. Take no heed of that, Dan Robbins was as straight as they come in things like that, he didn't side with anyone. He may not have acted as swiftly as some folk would have liked, but he had his reasons.'

'And what were his reasons for allowing Frank Heggerty, Slim Cairns and Jos McKay to remain free? They are all wanted men.'

'Now that I don't rightly know,' admitted Hal. 'He did say that seein' as how they wasn't wanted for murder or anythin' like that, and as long as they didn't cause no trouble in Goose Rapids, it was easier to pretend they didn't exist.'

Ellis hauled himself off the bed and sighed. 'That, my young friend, is one of the biggest problems I, as a marshal, have with most sheriffs. It seems to me that as long as there's no trouble to themselves they're only too ready to turn the other way.'

'Didn't you ever do that?' asked Hal, although he already really knew the answer.

'No!' replied Ellis very firmly. 'If you ever want to make anythin' more of yourself than an also-ran sheriff from some backwoods town that nobody has ever heard of, you won't do it either.'

'I hear what you say, Mr Stack,' smiled Hal. 'I only hope I can live up to it.'

THREE

'I trust you had a good night's sleep,' greeted Mayor O'Hara rather sarcastically as Marshal Ellis Stack entered the mayor's office. 'I must say I had thought you would have taken the trouble to visit me last night. I remained here, in this office until just after ten.'

'I did say I'd let you know if there was anything I wanted from you,' reminded Ellis. 'I talked with your sheriff, Hal Gibson most of the evening establishing exactly what happened.'

'Which is something I could have told you. I would point out that Hal Gibson, as keen as he might be, is not an experienced sheriff. He has been deputy for just under two years and, as far as this town is concerned, is at present acting purely as a temporary sheriff.'

'Then you'd better make him permanent as soon as possible,' said Ellis. 'He's a good man.'

'Is that some sort of order?' huffed O'Hara. 'Since when have the marshal's office had the power to dictate to anyone just who they must have as sheriff?'

Ellis sighed and smiled thinly as he sat himself down, unasked, in a large, comfortable leather chair and not the hard-backed chair obviously put out for him. 'Mr Mayor, I think you and I had better get one thing straight. I am not here to tell you how to run your town or to tell you who should be your sheriff. I am just passing a personal opinion that Hal Gibson is the ideal man for the job. As for other matters, I do have the authority to conduct an investigation into the death of your previous sheriff, Dan Robbins, just as I have the right to investigate any murder. I am not interested in any petty squabbles you may have and I am not really interested in the bad blood between Sam Paxton and William Gray, just as long as they don't break state or federal law.'

'Then use your authority and arrest the men responsible,' retorted the mayor. 'Why, even I can see that it's as plain as the nose on your face that it was either Frank Heggerty or Slim Cairns.'

'Or Jeremiah Paxton, or James Gray,' reminded Ellis.

'Heggerty and Cairns are outlaws!' insisted O'Hara. 'For all their faults, Jeremiah and James are from well-established and respected families in this territory.'

'Heggerty and Cairns may be wanted for robbery and assault,' agreed Ellis, 'but that doesn't make them killers. Nor does being from a good family mean a man can't be a killer. There was a case last year of a man murderin' a storekeeper just 'cos he was short of cash and his father was a judge.'

'Words!' snorted O'Hara. 'If you can't see that one of them is responsible, especially since I, myself, heard them threaten

Robbins, then I must question how and why you are a marshal.'

'Not by arrestin' the first person anyone suggests,' said Ellis. 'You run your town, Mr Mayor, just leave me to do my business in my own way.'

'Marshal, there are three men out there who are wanted criminals,' said O'Hara trying to sound very official. 'I would suggest that it is your duty, as a United States marshal, to arrest those men and ensure that they stand trial, if not for the murder of Dan Robbins, which one or all of them are implicated in in my opinion, then for those crimes of which they do stand accused.'

Ellis had to admit that the mayor did have a very good point. There was no reason why he should not arrest the men, although instinct told him that by doing so it would only hinder the investigations into the death of Sheriff Dan Robbins. Whether the mayor was right or not, Ellis certainly was not going to allow some petty official of some town nobody had ever heard of dictate to him what he must and must not do.

He did think about confronting O'Hara with the suggestion that either he or his wife might have committed the murder but he decided that for the moment that knowledge was best kept to himself.

'I'll think about it,' agreed Ellis. 'I don't think they're goin' anywhere for the moment, it'll keep. Now, if you've nothing else to say to me or tell me, I'll get about the business of finding out just who murdered Dan Robbins.' He rose, replaced his hat and nodded curtly. 'Good morning to you, Mr Mayor, I'll keep you informed of anything I think you need to know.'

The mayor watched helplessly as Ellis clattered out of the room and down the stairs – the mayor's office being situated on the upper floor of the small building which served as offices of the town council – and resolved to call a meeting of the council to discuss the marshal's attitude.

Ellis had arranged to meet Hal Gibson

outside the offices and the young sheriff was waiting as Ellis stomped out on to the boardwalk. 'I'd say O'Hara tried to give you a hard time,' grinned Hal. 'He's like that, likes to show everyone just how important he is, not that most folk take that much notice unless it suits them.'

'He tried,' conceded Ellis. 'He does have one fair point though, about Heggerty, Cairns and McKay.'

'About them still bein' free?' grinned Hal. 'Sure, he tried that with Mr Robbins and then me. Mr Robbins just ignored him, he always did. I didn't know for sure what to do so I told him I wasn't doin' nothin' till you arrived.'

'I think we'd better ride out and have words with those three,' said Ellis.

'Just words?' asked Hal.

'For the moment, I think so,' nodded Ellis.

The rider raced into the small paddock surrounding the house, leapt off his horse at the same time calling for his employer. Sam

Paxton appeared at the door, rifle in hand.

'What the hell is all the noise about?' he demanded. 'I thought we were bein' attacked or somethin'.'

'Hal Gibson and the marshal!' panted the man. 'Comin' here, they should be here in about ten minutes.'

'I'd've been surprised if they hadn't come,' replied Paxton, placing his rifle just inside the door. 'Thanks anyhow, now get back to work as if nothin' has happened.'

'I ... I just thought that maybe Frank Heggerty ought to know,' wheezed the man. 'They is liable to be arrested.'

'A distinct possibility,' smiled Paxton. 'Don't worry, I'll see to it.' The man nodded, remounted and rode off to his chores. Frank Heggerty and Jos McKay appeared at the door of the bunkhouse on the other side of the yard. 'You heard what he said,' said Paxton. 'The marshal is on his way. It's decision time for you. Stay and you may well be arrested and face prison or run and be branded murderers.'

The two men looked at each other and nodded briefly. 'We ain't about to run,' said McKay, 'but we ain't about to give up that easy either. You just tell him that we're out roundin' up strays or somethin'. We'll be up in that loft over there.'

'Where's Cairns?' called Paxton as the two raced to a barn.

'Ain't seen him all mornin',' came the reply. 'He'll have to look after himself.'

There was no time for Sam Paxton to worry himself just where the third of his hired guns was, Sheriff Hal Gibson and Marshal Ellis Stack were already approaching the house, a good five minutes before they were expected. Paxton seated himself on the porch and waited.

'Mornin' young Hal,' greeted Sam Paxton. He nodded to the other man but made no attempt to rise from the wicker chair. 'We ain't met, but I'd say you are Marshal Ellis Stack...' Ellis nodded and raised his hat slightly in mock salute. 'Your reputation goes before you, Marshal,' continued Paxton, 'even a hick town like Goose Rapids has heard of you.'

'Nice town,' conceded Ellis as he dismounted. 'Sort of place that time just passes by for the most part I'd say.'

'That's how it used to be,' admitted Paxton. 'Now, suddenly all hell has broken loose. Now I'm sure you didn't ride out all this way just to be sociable, Marshal. Please...' He indicated two other chairs. 'Sit down an' cool off, it's a hot day.' He called back into the house and a moment later a young Mexican woman arrived carrying a tray with three glasses and a large jug which she placed on a nearby table. 'Lemonade,' announced Paxton. 'Best lemonade you ever tasted.'

'Don't mind if I do,' agreed Ellis. Hal Gibson too gave a slight nod as the two lawmen joined the rancher on the porch. 'Seems like you were expecting us,' added Ellis.

Sam Paxton laughed. 'It's all open country

between Goose Rapids and here. You were seen twenty minutes ago.' He nodded to the girl who poured out the lemonade, handed a glass to each man and then withdrew into the house. 'Let me guess,' Paxton continued with a wry smile, 'You've come out here to arrest three men I employ.'

'I dare say the governor could find some law which says that you should not knowingly employ known outlaws,' said Ellis.

'I'm not a lawyer,' nodded Paxton. 'It is possible I suppose. Is that some sort of threat, Marshal? There's no need for that, I am a law-abiding citizen and you have my full co-operation.'

'Just a thought,' nodded Ellis sipping appreciatively at his lemonade. 'You're right about the lemonade, best I've tasted for a long time. Glad to hear you're willing to co-operate. Frank Heggerty, Slim Cairns and Jos McKay, I'd like to have words with them.'

'Then I'm afraid you'll have to come back,' smiled Paxton. 'I sent them out up to the Talahoe Range to look for strays.'

'Talahoe Range?' queried Ellis.

'Yeh...' Paxton pointed to some distant hills. 'That's them over there, maybe fifteen miles.'

'Very convenient,' muttered Ellis. 'OK, you just make sure they're all here first thing in the mornin'. In the meantime, tell me about the bad blood between you an' William Gray.'

'What's to tell?' shrugged Paxton. 'If you were a cattle man you'd understand these things happen. There ain't no range war if that's what you're thinkin'.'

'You maybe heard that I did some time in prison,' said Ellis. 'Sure, it's no secret. I was sent there on account of me an' my pa were cattle men. We had a ranch, nothin' like the size of yours but it was a good ranch. Some bigger rancher decided he wanted our land but my pa wouldn't sell so one day we suddenly found ourselves with a few head that didn't belong to us and we were accused of rustlin'.'

'What happened to your pa?' asked Paxton.

'Ended up on the wrong end of a rope!'

'Sorry to hear that,' said Paxton. 'Sure, it's no secret I want Gray's land. I've got plans, big plans and I need to expand. I've gone just about as far to the west and south as I can but Gray owns the land to the east an' north. Now as far as I know it's a matter of public record that I have offered William Gray more'n a fair price for his land but so far he's refused. He's got that right of course, I'll not deny that. If you listen to gossip, Marshal, you'll hear that all I want really is his water supply and I'll be the first to admit that I do. That water is no more'n half a mile from my boundary. I need it for the cattle on that part of the ranch. As things are, they have to go almost five miles for not very good water.'

Ellis looked at Hal Gibson questioningly.

'He's right,' nodded Hal. 'I know Gray has been offered more'n a fair price.'

'And what about the suggestion that you

were preparing to take that water by force?' asked Ellis.

Paxton laughed. 'That was some stupid idea my son, Jeremiah and Frank Heggerty had. I soon stopped that.'

'And I hear that it was you who suggested that life would be a lot easier if Dan Robbins were out of the way,' continued Ellis.

Once again Paxton laughed. 'Didn't I once read that back in history somewhere in England, some king wished to be rid of some priest without literally wantin' him dead an' somebody thought they were doin' the king a favour by killin' the priest.'

'Wouldn't know about that,' said Ellis. 'I ain't never read no history books.'

'Well I did, long time ago but certain things stick. Sure, it was suggested, and seriously, by that stupid son of mine that Robbins be killed, but I was havin' none of that.'

'Maybe somebody thought they were doin' you a favour,' suggested Ellis. 'Somebody like your son!'

Sam Paxton's reaction to that suggestion rather surprised Ellis.

'I got me two boys, Marshal,' grinned Paxton. 'Jeremiah, he's the eldest an' Daniel. Daniel is the worker; he ain't afraid to get out there with the other hands and get dirty, in fact that's what he'd rather be doin'. Good business head too. Jeremiah...' he laughed loudly, 'Anythin' to avoid work. Naw, I ain't tryin' to just protect my stupid son, but he wouldn't have the guts to do anythin' like that.'

'He could have got someone else to do it,' said Ellis.

'Heggerty or Cairns?' said Paxton. 'Sure, that's possible, but somehow I don't see either of them gettin' involved in murder. Robbers they may be but murderers? No, I don't think so.'

'I still want to talk to them,' said Ellis. 'You just make sure that all three are here first thing in the mornin'.'

'Are you goin' to take them back to jail?'

'Maybe, maybe not,' smiled Ellis. 'They're wanted men, they shouldn't be surprised if I do.'

'I'll tell 'em,' nodded Paxton.

'Now I want to talk to James Gray,' said Ellis draining the last of the lemonade from his glass and refusing the offer of another. 'Many thanks. Tell whoever made this it is the best I've ever tasted.'

Sam Paxton made no effort to move as his visitors mounted their horses but he did raise his glass in salute as they rode off. A few minutes later Heggerty and McKay appeared.

'You heard?' asked Paxton.

'Not really,' said Heggerty, 'but we guessed that he wanted us to be here in the mornin'.'

'That's about the strength of it,' nodded Paxton. 'Mind you, it's up to you.'

'Prison or a charge of murder!' muttered Heggerty.

'Tough choice,' grinned Paxton.

'Mr Paxton!' grated Jos McKay, 'I'd say

you were enjoyin' this.'

'Oh, I am!' laughed Paxton. 'Now go find Cairns and tell him what's happened.'

The two men glared at their employer for a second and then stomped off into the bunkhouse. A few minutes later Jos McKay returned.

'Slim's gone,' he announced. 'All his things are missin', his bedroll, clothes, horse, everythin'.'

Sam Paxton smiled. 'So he's runnin' scared. Boys, it looks like you just found the killer of Dan Robbins.'

'I tell you I was too drunk to even stand up,' insisted James Gray as he faced the marshal across the large table. 'There must have been at least twenty people in the saloon. I never left the place all night; Jed, the bartender, he can confirm that as can all the others.'

'Don't worry, I'll ask him,' said Ellis.

'He didn't do it!' hissed William Gray. 'And I ain't sayin' that just 'cos he's my son.

Me an' Martha, we brought all our children up to be honest and God-fearin'. Why, ask any one of 'em what happened two years ago, ask young Hal here, he'd just been made deputy...'

Ellis looked questioningly at Hal Gibson.

'Adam...' said Hal, 'he's the one Mr Robbins killed, took it into his head to raid the safe in the Cattlemen's Association office. Would have got away with it too but Mr Gray here somehow found out an' made Adam confess. He needn't have done, there was no evidence against Adam, but he did. Anyhow Adam was put up on trial but the judge took pity on him an' let him off on condition that he never did anythin' so stupid again. He said it was only his age, fifteen he was then, which saved him from prison.'

'I guess it'd be easy enough to check on the story,' said Ellis.

'I already have,' said Hal. 'Everyone, includin' Jed, swears that James never left the room all night.'

'Not even to go to the privy?'

'Not even that,' grinned Hal. 'I know, I asked on account of I only have to have a glass of beer an' I'm runnin' back an' forth all night.'

'James Gray?' asked Hal Gibson as he and Ellis rode away from the Gray ranch.

'It sure doesn't look like it,' admitted Ellis. 'You know how it is though, somebody seems to be in the same place all night and everyone swears that he was. The trouble is they don't notice when someone like that slips away for a few minutes. He becomes sort of invisible. How far from the saloon was it to where Dan Robbins was found?'

'Right across the street,' said Hal. 'Thirty yards maybe.'

'Slip out the back door, down the side alley, across the street in the dark with nobody about, kill Dan Robbins an' slip back into the saloon. If anyone queries it, he says he's been out to the privy but nobody notices.'

'He was drunk, remember,' said Hal.

'He pretends he's drunk, up till the time he kills the sheriff,' said Ellis. 'After that he does get drunk.'

'The way you put it James Gray is as guilty as hell,' sighed Hal.

'I never said that's what did happen,' grinned Ellis. 'I just said it was possible.'

'How long has he been gone?' asked Ellis.

Sam Paxton had ridden into Goose Rapids later that afternoon, about six hours after Slim Cairns' disappearance had been noted. He had deliberately left it that long simply to give the man a good start. It was his idea that the marshal would be forced to go after him and the further away he was the longer it would take. Of course he did not tell Ellis that his disappearance had been discovered just after he and Hal Gibson had left the ranch.

'Since sometime early this mornin', I guess,' smiled Paxton. 'I thought he was with Heggerty and McKay out at the

Talahoe Range roundin' up strays, but they say they never saw him. We checked and found his horse and all his gear missin'. I thought I'd better tell you straight away.'

Ellis smiled a little ruefully. 'Just like the good citizen you are. Thanks Mr Paxton.'

'Looks like you found your killer,' grinned Paxton.

Ellis smiled briefly and grunted, but did not answer. Sam Paxton seemed quite pleased with himself as he left the sheriff's office and headed for the saloon.

Hal Gibson studied the marshal for a few moments and smiled. 'Now in the normal way of things I'd agree with Mr Paxton and say we've found the killer,' he said, 'but there's somethin' about the way you're lookin' that tells me you don't think so.'

'It could be he did do it,' said Ellis, thoughtfully playing with a pencil. 'It just strikes me as bein' a little too convenient though. A known outlaw suddenly takes off after the death of a sheriff. Fine, if that had been the case straight after Robbins was murdered I might have gone along with it, but why now? It's been eight days since it happened. Why leave it till now to run, especially since he must have known I was coming. No, sir, it's just a little too convenient for my likin'.'

Hal Gibson smiled. 'I always thought bein' a lawman was easy, just a matter of chasing outlaws. Looks like I was wrong.'

Ellis laughed and jabbed the pencil into the desk, breaking the point. 'Hal, chasin' outlaws is the easy part an' I agree that does take up a fair bit of the time. It's times like this what make the job really interestin', pittin' your wits against someone who thinks he's clever'n you.'

'Well Slim Cairns has done a runner,' said Hal. 'Are you goin' after him?'

'I would if I knew which way he'd gone,' grinned Ellis. 'You got any ideas?'

Hal shrugged. 'Could be any direction, I guess.'

'Precisely,' nodded Ellis. 'No, all we can do is notify every sheriff in the state and hope someone finds him. They usually do, even if they don't arrest him.'

'In the meantime?' asked Hal.

'In the meantime we carry on as if Slim Cairns had never existed, which should wipe the smile off Sam Paxton's face.'

FOUR

'Well, I agree with Sam Paxton,' said Mayor O'Hara slamming his fist down on his desk. 'Slim Cairns is our man. It appears that everyone in Goose Rapids can see that but you, Marshal.'

'I never said he wasn't our man,' said Ellis, lounging back in the leather chair. 'I've just got my doubts, that's all. Why the hell should he kill Dan Robbins? Give me one good reason and I'll willingly agree with you, but as I see it Cairns had absolutely nothing to gain, in fact he had more to lose. Sure, he's a wanted criminal, but not for murder. For what he's done so far he'd probably get no more'n five years in prison. The murder of a sheriff, or anyone for that matter, would get him hanged.'

'He was sore because Dan ordered him out of town,' replied O'Hara.

Ellis laughed. 'If you don't mind me sayin' so, Mr Mayor, that's just about the dumbest reason for killin' anyone. No, it's my opinion that Slim Cairns simply ran because he was scared of bein' arrested and sent to prison, not because he murdered Dan Robbins.'

'If you don't catch him you'll never find out,' insisted O'Hara. 'You should be out there huntin' him down right now.'

'Tell me which way he went and I might just do that,' said Ellis. 'As it is I don't make a move until I know.'

Mayor O'Hara sat back and stared sneeringly at Ellis for a short time, eventually he opened a drawer and took out a note which he handed to the marshal.

'I sent this wire this morning,' said O'Hara, still sneering. 'As you can see, I sent it to the governor requesting that you be replaced. The town council is far from satisfied that you are capable of doing the job you were sent here to do.'

'You've got that right,' smiled Ellis. 'OK, so replace me, don't you think I'd rather be at home with my wife and son?'

'It could cost you your job,' warned the mayor.

Ellis laughed and stood up, towering above O'Hara who visibly cowered as if expecting the marshal's huge fist to slam into his face. 'I think it'll take a bit more than a two-bit mayor from a hick town to take my job. Just as a thought, *Mr Mayor*, I've even got you marked down as a likely killer of Dan Robbins.'

This time O'Hara's expression changed to one of pure incredulity mixed with a certain amount of panic.

'Me!' he spluttered. 'Me! Now I know you

are totally unfit for the job. Have you been out in the sun without your hat? It would certainly appear that you have gone completely mad. I demand that you justify what you say.'

'Do I need to?' smiled Ellis, resting his hands on the desk and leaning forward slightly. 'Think about it, O'Hara.'

'I have no idea what you are talking about!' spluttered the mayor.

'Mrs O'Hara?' suggested Ellis. 'I'll say no more, but I think you know what I mean.'

'My wife!' exclaimed the mayor. 'What has she got to do with all this?'

Ellis stood up straight and went to the door. 'Now if you don't mind, I need to get back to the sheriff's office, he's gone out to bring Frank Heggerty and Jos McKay in. I decided that I couldn't afford to have them run out on me as well.'

Ellis slammed the door and clattered down the wooden stairs and out on to the street just in time to see Hal Gibson leading two horses with riders who had their hands tied behind their backs.

'Any problems?' asked Ellis as Hal drew near.

'None at all,' smiled Hal. 'They didn't even argue. I thought I'd better tie their hands though, just in case.'

Ellis nodded and spoke to Frank Heggerty. 'Maybe you should've run too, you had the chance.'

'And be branded a murderer?' replied Heggerty. 'No thanks, Marshal. I may have done some stupid things in my time but I ain't that stupid. I'll do my time in prison. I've done it before and I dare say I'll do it again, but at least I won't be dancin' on the end of a rope.'

'That goes for me too,' scowled McKay.

'Lock 'em up!' smiled Ellis. 'I'll be along later.'

'Marshal Stack!' A woman stood at the door of one of the grandest houses in Goose Rapids and Ellis instinctively knew her identity.

'Mrs O'Hara, ma'am,' he smiled raising his hat.

'You know who I am?' she asked, seeming surprised.

'An educated guess, you might say,' smiled Ellis. 'Yes, ma'am, what can I do for you?'

'You can come inside, I want to talk to you.' She held the door open and it was plain to Ellis that this was something more than a request, it was almost a presidential command.

Ellis entered the house and was shown into a large, extremely comfortably furnished room where, had Mr O'Hara been present, he would have had no hesitation in commandeering the most comfortable looking chair. As it was, he did not want to antagonize Mrs O'Hara in any way.

'Please, have a seat,' Mrs O'Hara offered.

'If it's all the same to you, ma'am,' said Ellis, 'I am kinda dirty. I don't want to spoil your covers.'

'Most considerate,' she smiled. She pulled

out a wooden, high-backed chair from behind a sofa and offered it to him. This time he accepted. 'Now, Marshal,' she said, not sitting down herself 'it would appear that you have somewhat upset my husband.'

'Upset?' queried Ellis as if not knowing what she was hinting at. 'I guess it's me who should be upset, he sent a wire to the governor complainin' about me.'

Mrs O'Hara smiled and nodded. 'That's typical of Thomas, he always acts first and thinks later. Please don't be obtuse with me, Mr Stack...'

'If I knew what that meant, I wouldn't be,' smiled Ellis.

'Among other things, it means dim-witted,' she said. 'Whatever else you may be, Marshal, you are not dim-witted.'

'That's not everybody's opinion,' said Ellis.

'This morning, in my husband's office, you told him that even he is a suspect for the murder of Dan Robbins...'

'He told you?'

'He didn't have to, I was in the adjoining room,' she replied. 'Oh, he didn't know I was there, I had gone in just before he came into his office. There is a door between the two rooms, perhaps you noticed?' Ellis nodded. 'I confess that I was listening at the door,' she continued. 'Now, exactly what did you mean when you hinted that it might concern me?'

Ellis sighed and shook his head. He decided that he would tell her what he had been told. 'You and Dan Robbins were havin' an affair,' he said.

'If nothing else, you are direct,' she smiled, 'and I shall be as direct with you. You are quite right, Dan and I were, as you put it, having an affair. As a matter of fact we had been having this affair on and off for more than four years. I won't go into the details, they are of no concern to this case nor to you. Tell me, how did you, a complete stranger to Goose Rapids, find out about Dan and me? I am quite certain that nobody else even thought it possible.'

'Except one,' smiled Ellis.

'Ah, Hal Gibson,' she smiled nodding her head. 'Now there's a nice boy, well mannered, honest, reliable...'

'And knows when to keep his mouth shut,' added Ellis.

'That too,' she agreed. 'I wonder how long he has known?'

'About two years,' said Ellis. 'The thing is, does your husband know?'

Mrs O'Hara stared out of the window a little dreamily. 'You know, I do believe he does. He's never said anything of course, but yes, I do believe he does.'

'And does it bother you?'

'Oh no, not in the least.' She sat down opposite Ellis. 'Just for your information, Marshal, not that it is the slightest concern of yours, Thomas O'Hara would be out on the streets without a penny if it wasn't for me. I own everything, this house, the saloon, the drapery store – in fact I own most of Goose Rapids. Yes, Marshal, it's my money, Thomas does what I tell him to do.'

Somehow Ellis was not surprised, having now seen Mrs O'Hara. He had rapidly formed the opinion that she was a calculating woman who always had her own way. It just puzzled him as to why she should risk gossip by having an affair with someone like Dan Robbins.

'Dan Robbins?' he asked.

She smiled. 'Dan and I go back a long way. We almost married, but he had some sort of stupid pride which wouldn't allow him to marry a woman more wealthy than he was. Maybe it was as well, he never had much ambition. I'm not really sure just how our affair started, it just sort of happened although neither of us had any intention of taking it further, which is why it was an on-and-off affair.'

'Could your husband have killed Dan Robbins?'

She laughed. 'I doubt it, he comes over all funny if he has to kill a cockroach. I see what you mean though, jealousy. Mmmm ... it would be nice to think of two men fighting to the death for my hand but no, I don't think so. Thomas knows where he stands and he likes his lifestyle too much to do anything about my er ... indiscretions.'

'I take it that means there have been others?' said Ellis.

'You can take it how you like, Marshal, I don't really care. Now, I thank you for sparing me your valuable time. If there is anything I can do to help you, please ask. Now I must bid you good afternoon.'

'One more thing,' said Ellis as he stood up to leave. 'Could you, indeed, did you kill Dan Robins?'

She laughed again. 'As to whether I could, I think so. As to whether I did? Why do you ask?'

'Maybe he was becoming too demanding, especially since his wife died. Maybe he wanted somethin' more than just an affair.'

She laughed louder. 'Now I am a prime suspect! How delightful. Did I murder my lover? That's something you must find out, Marshal.'

'Oh for a nice easy chase across a desert after a bunch of wild outlaws!' sighed Ellis as he entered the sheriff's office.

'Things not going too well?' asked Hal Gibson.

'Suspects are comin' out of the woodwork thicker'n ants out of an ant-hill,' replied Ellis. 'Have those two said anythin' yet?'

'Just one thing,' said Hal. He produced a gold crucifix on a chain. 'They say it belongs to Slim Cairns and that whatever else he may leave behind or forget, he would never leave this. It apparently belonged to his mother.'

'Where was it?'

'On the floor, by his bunk,' said Hal.

'So this time he couldn't find it but decided he had to get out quick.'

'My idea too,' grinned Hal, 'but they don't think so.'

'I'd better have words with them,' sighed Ellis.

He went through the door which led to the

two cells and confronted the two outlaws with the crucifix.

'We don't think Slim ran out,' said Jos McKay. 'The three of us have been together for a long time and wherever Slim went, that crucifix went. He lost it once when we'd robbed a bank and insisted on goin' back for it. Almost got us killed but he wouldn't leave it behind. That's why we don't think he's run off.'

'So where is he then?' asked Ellis. 'How do you explain his other things missin'?'

'We don't,' said Heggerty, 'but we do know that Slim ain't run out. Hell, he was sayin' that it would be stupid an' that we'd be hunted as murderers.'

'That's all I need!' sighed Ellis. 'OK, so he's still around somewhere. Have you got any ideas?'

'Just one,' said Heggerty. 'Slim had found himself a woman somewheres. She must have been somethin', I ain't never seen him in such a state before.'

'Who is she?'

asked, fixing Gray with one of his official stares.

James Gray cowered slightly and fumbled with his hat. 'I did go into town that night fully intent on killing Dan Robbins,' he said. 'Sure, I admit that much. Only problem is someone beat me to it.'

'So it appears,' sighed Ellis. 'How did you intend to kill him?'

'Same way as whoever did do it did, with a knife,' said Gray. 'Hear me out, Marshal. I wasn't that drunk when Dan came on his round, I was just pretendin'...'

Ellis turned to Hal Gibson who was at another table nearby. 'Now ain't that just what I said,' he smiled. 'OK, carry on.'

'I saw Dan makin' his rounds the second time, just about midnight, that's when I slipped out the back, down the alley an' across the street.'

'You must have some kind of crystal ball,' said Hal Gibson. 'That's word for word how you said it would be.'

Ellis smiled a little smugly. 'And when you

went into the alley Dan Robbins was already dead.'

'That's just about it,' sighed Gray. 'I guess I just sort of lost my nerve. I knew that if anyone found me or I told anyone they'd immediately think it was me so I just got back to the saloon and after that I really did get drunk. The biggest surprise I had was when everybody said I'd never left the room all night, not even to go to the privy.'

'You'd become part of the furniture,' said Ellis.

'I still don't get it,' said Gray. 'Anyhow, that's it, Marshal, that's how it was, but I didn't murder him.'

'You say you saw Robbins go into the alley,' said Ellis. 'If you didn't kill him then whoever did must have been there. Did you see anyone?'

Gray thought for a moment. 'You know, I hadn't thought of that. That alley is a dead end, ain't no way out. Dan used to check the back door of the Cattlemen's office, that's the only door down there.'

'Now that we don't know,' grinned McKay. 'That's the honest truth. I hope you're goin' to put in a good word for us with the judge seein' as how we've been so helpful.'

'I'll think about it,' smiled Ellis.

'Now what does he want?' sighed Ellis as he sat at the desk toying with the crucifix.

James Gray was standing at the door obviously deciding whether to open it or not. Eventually he did open it and, doffing his hat, cautiously approached the marshal.

'Marshal,' croaked Gray. 'I guess I got some sort of confession to make.'

'Confession!' sighed Ellis. 'Don't tell me you've come to admit to the murder of Dan Robbins?'

'No, sir, well, not exactly that is,' mumbled Gray.

Ellis placed the crucifix in a drawer and indicated that his visitor should sit in the chair on the other side of the desk.

'Now what does not exactly mean?' he

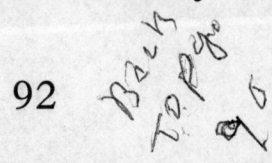

'Did you see or hear anythin'?' repeated Ellis.

James Gray became very thoughtful. 'Yeh, now you come to mention it, I did hear somethin', but I was too scared to take that much notice. There was a funny sound. I guess the nearest I can say is someone draggin' a piece of cloth across a floor. Yeh, that's it.'

'A piece of cloth?' asked Ellis. 'Is that all?'

'That's all, Marshal,' said Gray. 'Sorry I can't be more helpful, but you've got to believe me, I didn't kill Dan Robbins.'

'Seems like a day for confessions,' said Ellis as he once again saw a figure hesitating at the office door. 'Here comes your mayor.'

'Confession?' queried Hal Gibson.

'From the way he's lookin' I don't think it's anythin' official. Maybe it'd be better if you weren't around.'

'It's about time I made my round,' grinned Hal. He raised his hat to the mayor as they passed each other at the door and O'Hara waited until the young sheriff was out of sight before approaching Ellis.

'Take a seat,' Ellis invited, indicating the wooden chair on the opposite side of the desk. 'Sorry we ain't got anythin' more comfortable.'

O'Hara mumbled something which Ellis could not make out and then sat down and stared hard at the marshal. He produced what was obviously a telegraph message and studied it.

'It would appear that the governor has total faith in you and your methods, I only wish I could share his views.' He crumpled the piece of paper and pushed it into his pocket. 'However, that is not what I came here to talk to you about.' Ellis smiled, stretched back in his chair and nodded. 'First of all,' continued O'Hara, 'I demand to know exactly what you meant when you made reference to my wife and the possibility that it was I who murdered Dan Robbins.'

Ellis sighed slightly and gazed at the

ceiling. Eventually he lowered his gaze and looked at the mayor. 'You know as well as I do that your wife was having an affair with Dan Robbins. I think you have known for a long time but did nothing about it.'

O'Hara gulped slightly and nodded self-consciously. 'I must admit that you do seem very efficient, Marshal. Yes, indeed I did know about the so-called affair between my wife and the sheriff. I went along with it because it was hardly anything very serious. As far as they were both concerned it was nothing more than a brief distraction. They would go for months without seeing each other – except in the normal course of things – and suddenly they would see each other regularly for a few weeks.'

'Normally, I would have thought it very strange that any man, especially a man of your standing in the community, would tolerate such behaviour from his wife,' said Ellis, 'but since it appears that it is you who are completely dependent upon your wife, I understand your hesitation and tolerance.'

The mayor gazed at Ellis in pure amazement. 'How on earth did you find that out?'

'It's no secret,' grinned Ellis, 'your wife told me.'

'Good God!' muttered O'Hara. 'Has that woman no shame?'

Ellis leaned forward and rested his arms on the desk. 'Is that all you came to see me about?'

'What? ... oh, oh no,' faltered O'Hara. 'It's just that.... Hell, it doesn't matter, I'm sorry to have bothered you. Good day to you, Marshal!' He stood and dashed for the door, slamming it shut behind him. Ellis mused to himself. It was plain that the mayor had something on his mind.

I'll find out, Ellis said to himself.

'Are you quite certain that this is the same crucifix that belongs to Slim Cairns?' Ellis was quizzing the two men in the cells again. 'It doesn't look like anythin' special, somethin' that could be bought almost anywhere.'

'That's Slim's all right,' assured Heggerty.

'It's got the name "Alice" on the back.'

'Alice!' said Ellis, turning it over, although he knew very well that it did. 'I take it Alice was his mother.'

'That's right,' said Heggerty, 'he had been devoted to her and it was the only thing he had of hers.'

'And now he's found himself another woman,' said Ellis. 'Did either of you ever meet his mother?'

'No, she'd died long before he took up with us,' said Jos McKay.

'Pity, I don't suppose there was a picture or anythin'?'

'Not that we know of,' said McKay. 'Why all this interest in his mother?'

'It was just a thought,' said Ellis. 'I wondered if this woman he'd met looked anything like his mother.'

The two outlaws looked at each other briefly. 'As a matter of fact, he did say somethin' like that I seem to remember,' said Heggerty. 'Just like Ma! That's what he said. Oh, an' there's just one more thing: I know we said he'd found himself a woman an' as far as it goes that's true, but we don't think the woman was havin' anythin' to do with him.'

'Interesting,' said Ellis. 'Are you sure about that?'

'Not completely,' said McKay, 'but we sure got that impression.'

Ellis played with the crucifix for a moment, smiling to himself. 'I wonder!' he muttered.

'You are, of course, completely mad!' declared Mrs O'Hara. 'I will admit that one of those dreadful outlaws was paying me undue attention, but I certainly did not give him any encouragement. I don't even know his name.'

'Slim Cairns,' said Ellis.

'The one who escaped?' responded Mrs O'Hara. 'Perhaps here you have your murderer, Mr Stack. If the man was so besotted with me, he could have found out about Dan Robbins and me and, in some sort of jealous fit, decided to eliminate the man he saw as a rival.'

Ellis sighed heavily. Just such a thought had entered his head, but it made him feel quite depressed to hear someone else say it. He had no more questions to ask Mrs O'Hara and left her smiling to herself and preening her hair. He was now even more convinced that she was a woman who enjoyed the attention of men and probably even encouraged their attentions. As to whether such encouragement would extend to a rather scruffy outlaw and ranch hand such as Slim Cairns was another matter, although he would not have been too surprised.

'I am rapidly coming to the conclusion that if I ask enough questions and delve deeply enough, I could find a reason why almost everyone in this town wanted to kill Dan Robbins,' said Ellis, slamming his pencil down on the desk and screwing up a list he had been making. 'Not only that, it seems that almost anyone could have had the opportunity.'

Hal Gibson smiled as he sipped a mug of coffee. 'From what I've heard, my feelin's are that the answer is Slim Cairns. I don't know his reason but that's the way it seems to me.'

'Too easy!' muttered Ellis. 'I know I said that before, but I'll say it again, a known outlaw on the run, a dead sheriff ... all the right ingredients but as far as I'm concerned the mixture don't taste right.'

'Too easy?' laughed Hal. 'Maybe that's your trouble, Mr Stack, you're lookin' for somethin' complicated which just ain't there.'

FIVE

The buckboard crunched to a halt outside the sheriff's office, creating a cloud of dust as the brake was applied firmly by a strong arm which would have done credit to any man. The wheel skidded and almost before the buckboard had stopped, a short, fat, skirted figure leapt off and confronted Ellis as he left the office.

'Caroline Gray,' announced the woman as she barred his way. 'We met out at the ranch the other day.'

Ellis would normally have raised his hat when greeting a lady, but on this occasion he felt that such a show of manners would have been completely lost on her. Instead he just smiled and allowed himself to be forced against the wall as she closed in on him. Not that he had much choice in the matter. Short she might have been but her bulk made argument most difficult.

'Miss Gray!' smiled Ellis. 'Nice to see you again. What can I do for you?'

'Ain't what you can do for me, Marshal,' she grinned. 'It's maybe somethin' I can do for you.' She looked about at the few curious faces and laughed. 'Best go inside, too many folk about here who're interested in other folk's business.'

Ellis agreed that it might be better if they did go inside the office and opened the door for her. She marched in and immediately commandeered the one comfortable chair, the one behind Ellis's desk. He chose not to point out her mistake and sat himself on the corner of the desk and looked down at her. It was his way of establishing his dominance, although it seemed plain that she did not notice.

'Now, just what is it that might be of use to me?' he asked.

'I'll come to that,' she said, seeming to test the chair for strength as she bounced in it. 'First, I hear my brother came to see you an' confessed that he'd set out that night to kill Dan Robbins.' Ellis nodded. 'Damn stupid thing to do ... confess that that's what he was goin' to do. I told him not to be so damn fool stupid an' keep his mouth shut, but it was Pa who said he ought to go an' see you, damned fool pair. That's my pa through an' through though, too damned honest for his own good sometimes.'

'It's a pity there aren't more who think the same,' said Ellis.

'Not out here,' asserted Caroline. 'It's dog-eat-dog out here, Marshal, you ought to know that. Still, that ain't no concern of yours. The thing is, James didn't do it even if he admits he was goin' to. If he said the sheriff was dead when he got there, then that's how it was.'

'I have not made up my mind one way or the other,' said Ellis. 'Now, one thing I am quite certain of is that you didn't ride out here just to tell me your brother is innocent.'

'Too damned right I didn't,' grinned Caroline. 'I had to come into town anyhow so I decided to tell you.'

'Tell me what?' sighed Ellis.

'I've known for three days now, ever since he ran off...'

'Known what for three days and since who ran off?'

'Slim Cairns, of course!' exclaimed Caroline. 'Who else?'

'Who else indeed?' Ellis sighed again.

Caroline looked at him as though he were simple. 'Slim Cairns ran out three days ago, right?' Ellis nodded. 'Now I don't know why he ran off, 'ceptin' maybe he's the one what murdered the sheriff, but that don't make sense to me. If he had killed Robbins I reckon a man like that would've run for it as soon as it happened.'

'Unless he was being paid for the murder,' suggested Ellis.

Caroline laughed. 'Who the hell would want to pay a man like that to kill the sheriff? He gets caught an' blabs an' whoever it was is in deep trouble. It would've made sense if someone had hired him an' then killed him after he'd murdered the sheriff ... I hope I ain't goin' too fast for you, Marshal, I knows you lawmen ain't too quick when it comes to usin' your brain.'

Ellis ignored the last remark but the rest of what she said made perfect sense and he silently cursed himself for not thinking about it before. However, he did not let her know that she had talked sense.

'All very interesting,' Ellis said, 'but what is the point of it all? Nobody knows better than I do that Slim Cairns has made a run for it.'

Caroline sighed heavily in apparent disgust. 'Maybe I ain't makin' myself too clear, Marshal. I'll try an' put in words even you can understand. Slim Cairns runs off – why, we don't know for certain – but has he? No, he damned well hasn't. Sure, he's skipped town, either gettin' away from you or, more likely, someone else. The thing is he hasn't run off. All he's done is pretend he has. He wants someone to think he has. You with me so far, Marshal?' Ellis nodded. 'Good!' she continued. 'Now the thing is, I know where he is an' he don't know I know.'

'You know where Slim Cairns is right now?' said Ellis.

Caroline laughed. 'See, if you listen hard enough, even you can understand. That's what I said, I know where Slim Cairns is right now. Leastways if it ain't Cairns then there's someone hidin' out who is his double.'

'And he doesn't know?' prompted Ellis.

'Pretty damned sure he don't,' she asserted. 'I ain't got that close.'

Ellis thought about the crucifix and wondered if Cairns would be foolish enough to hang about just for that. From what he had heard from Heggerty and McKay, it was just possible, although Ellis had his doubts.

'Where?' he asked.

'Up in Symmington Valley,' she replied. 'There's some caves up there, that's where he's holed up.'

'Symmington Valley could be on the moon as far as I'm concerned,' smiled Ellis, 'but I expect I'll find it.'

'Part of our land,' explained Caroline, 'not that anyone goes up there that much. It ain't no use for cattle grazin' an' nothin' grows up there. Don't know why Pa ever bought it. Just head north out of Goose Rapids, take a left where the Goose River an' Bull Creek join an' just keep followin' the creek till you come to Symmington Valley. There ain't no missin' it, you'll know when you're there.'

'How far?'

Caroline thought for a moment. 'Distance don't mean much as far as I'm concerned an' most folks is the same. It's about half a day's steady ridin'.'

It was quite true, people tended not to think of where or how far something was in terms of miles but in riding times. It was a criterion Ellis tended to use himself.

'Have you told anyone else about this?' he asked.

'Nope!' she replied firmly. 'It don't pay to tell most folk nothin', not even the time of day.'

'What about your pa or your brothers?'

'I ain't told them neither,' she grinned. 'Just 'cos they is kin don't mean I trust 'em any more'n the next man. The way they're all fired up right now they'd ride on up there an' have themselves a neck-tie party.'

'And why should that bother you?' asked Ellis.

For the first time, Caroline Gray blushed, or at least she appeared to under the general grime on her face. 'Hell, Marshal,' she grinned, 'look at me. I ain't exactly no picture now am I? Five foot two an' almost that round. Only man ever to show an interest in me up till now was old Ted Fisher an' all he wanted was a housekeeper. He must be thirty years older'n me.'

'Up till now?' smiled Ellis. 'I take it that means that Slim Cairns did show some interest in you?'

Caroline appeared to blush again. 'Could say that, Marshal. Leastways he's the only man what ever showed any interest in my body, only man what has ever wanted to make love to me.'

'And did he?' smiled Ellis.

'I ain't complainin',' grinned Caroline.

Try as he might Ellis simply could not visualize Caroline Gray in the role of the mother of Slim Cairns. 'OK, that's your business I guess,' grinned Ellis. 'There's just one thing. Did he ever talk to you about his mother or about any woman who reminded him of his mother?'

She looked at him slightly mystified for a moment and then smiled. 'Come to think of it, he did say that there was some woman in town who looked exactly like his mother. He never said who though, but it sure weren't me, he told me that much.'

'Thanks,' said Ellis, 'you did the right thing in coming to me but I am still slightly troubled. If you and he were that close, why haven't you just warned him?'

'That's easy,' she grinned. 'I almost talked him into giving himself up to you an' doin' his time in prison. We was close enough to talk about gettin' hitched but I ain't prepared to take up with no outlaw. I'll take him an' gladly once he's paid for what he's done. I reckon Pa would even take him on on the ranch. I think he was just about to do that but then suddenly somethin' made him run.'

'Any idea what?'

'Not really, 'ceptin' I have this feelin' it

concerned this other woman you was talkin' about, the one who looked like his mother.'

Ellis resolved to ask Mrs O'Hara just what had transpired between Slim Cairns and herself, although he doubted that he would get a satisfactory answer. Perhaps the best way to resolve the question was to ask Slim Cairns himself.

As Ellis had expected, Mrs O'Hara had been singularly uncooperative when asked about Slim Cairns, other than to confirm once again that he had been showing an unnatural interest in her. She flatly denied that there was any sort of liaison or point of mutual interest between them and, with no other evidence to back him up, Ellis was forced to abandon that line of questioning, for the moment at least.

His mind turned over all the possibilities and permutations as he struck out north following the course of Bull Creek, a deep-sided gully with a shallow stream flowing through it. One of the possibilities was that

Slim Cairns did murder Dan Robbins, but such a possibility was not very high up Ellis's list. Apart from the chance that Cairns was paid to kill the sheriff, there was no real reason why he should. Slim Cairns was not wanted for murder and Ellis felt that it was most unlikely that he would do something so stupid. However, the possibility remained that someone had paid – or agreed to pay – Slim Cairns to carry out the killing. If it was the case and Cairns had not been paid, then it gave a reason for his remaining in the area.

The involvement of Cairns was just one aspect amongst what seemed a neverending list of suspects and chances to carry out the killing. On the one hand James Gray had admitted that he had intended to do just that but claimed that someone had beaten him to it. Ellis could remember hearing of someone who admitted something similar and made the claim that someone else had done it, only to finally admit that he had carried out the murder.

So, something similar was possible with James Gray.

His other suspects included Mayor O'Hara, Mrs O'Hara and even the men now held in jail. After a time he decided that too much thinking was making his head hurt so he tried to forget, not very successfully.

As predicted, Ellis found himself in what he assumed to be Symmington Valley at about noon and, as Caroline Gray had told him, it was high, wide and barren. The caves, he had been told, were about a mile into the valley, set about half-way into the cliff face with a narrow trail leading to them. What he had not been told was that it was impossible to approach the caves without being seen or to get even within rifle shot distance of them.

Once he had established just where the caves were, Ellis settled himself behind a large rock some 200 yards away, took out his spyglass and watched. At first he thought that his quarry must have fled since there was no movement at all for at least half an hour, but, quite suddenly, a figure appeared and seemed to be looking in Ellis's direction.

Ellis decided that his best plan was to show himself and then try to talk the man down and accordingly walked slowly forward, his arms held high and wide to show that he meant no harm. Cairns allowed him to get within calling range before firing a warning shot. Ellis stood where he was, knowing that had he wanted to, Slim Cairns could have killed him.

'We've got to talk!' called Ellis.

'Ain't got nothin' to talk about,' replied Cairns. 'All you got to know is I didn't kill the sheriff.'

'I never said you did,' shouted Ellis. 'All the more reason we've got to talk, I think you know who did.'

This observation brought loud laughter from Cairns. 'That's just where you're wrong, Marshal. I don't know nothin' about that. In fact you've got this whole thing wrong, all of you, you all got it wrong.'

'Then come back with me and tell me what the truth is,' suggested Ellis.

'The truth is I didn't have nothin' to do with murderin' Dan Robbins. Anyhow, Marshal, how the hell did you know I was up here?'

'Caroline Gray,' called Ellis. 'She knew you were up here. Don't ask me how, but she does. I gather you an' her have been pretty close.'

'Could say that!' barked Cairns. 'Stupid bitch!' he oathed. 'I thought her an' me ... well, that don't matter. Just goes to show you can never trust a woman.'

'Does that include Mrs O'Hara?'

Cairns appeared to be thinking about that and it took him about two minutes to reply. 'She's a bitch too, just like the rest of 'em. I thought she was different, looked just like my ma. That's where it ended though, just looked like her.'

'For what it's worth, Cairns,' called Ellis, 'I don't think you did kill Dan Robbins, but I think you know somethin' which could tell me who did.'

'Don't know nothin!' shouted Cairns. 'Maybe you don't think I killed him, Marshal, but it's what a jury says what counts an' from what I seen about the folk in Goose Rapids, they'd convict a new-born baby of it if they could, just so's they could get back to what they call normal livin'.'

'They can only put you on trial if you are charged with murder,' Ellis pointed out. 'Sure, you'll probably serve five years for what you've done so far, maybe less if I speak up for you, you know, tell the court how you helped me find Dan Robbins's murderer.'

'You make it sound too easy, Marshal,' replied Cairns. 'Why should I trust you?'

'Dan Robbins never tried to arrest you,' said Ellis.

'No, but he would've done if he'd been allowed to,' laughed Cairns. 'He was just like the rest of 'em, anythin' for the easy life. He told us to get out of town an' he meant it an' that's just what we was about to do when he was killed.'

'I believe you,' called Ellis. 'Come back with me an' make a statement and I guarantee you won't be charged with murder.'

Cairns appeared to falter but then he disappeared into one of the caves with the warning that Ellis was not to make a move towards them. Ellis stood his ground and waited.

For two hours, Ellis sat on a rock staring up at the cave entrance waiting for something to happen and when it did, he had to confess that he was surprised.

Slim Cairns suddenly appeared at the entrance of a different cave leading his horse. Ellis did not move until horse and rider were at the bottom of the track on flatter ground. Even then he did not make any threatening move towards Cairns as the outlaw rode slowly towards him.

'I'm glad you seen some sense,' said Ellis, turning and leading the way to where he had left his horse. 'Maybe now we can get some sort of logic into this situation.'

'I'm trustin' you, Marshal,' hissed Cairns as he rode behind. 'I ain't never trusted a lawman in my life, 'ceptin' once when I was a boy an' that got me a good whippin'.'

'And why me?' asked Ellis.

'You know what it's like to be accused of somethin' you didn't do,' explained Cairns, 'an' I do hear that you is just about the fairest lawman there is.'

'I like to think so,' smiled Ellis. 'What happened when you were a kid?'

'So long ago I don't really remember,' admitted Cairns. 'Somethin' to do with stealin' from a general store, which I didn't do. Long an' short of it was I got me a good whippin' for it all on the say-so of a no-good sheriff.'

'I know the feelin',' nodded Ellis as he rode ahead of the outlaw. He had deliberately chosen to ride in front as a way of showing Cairns that he could be trusted. 'More to the point, just why did you choose to run when you must've known it would make it appear that you had killed Dan Robbins?'

Cairns laughed cynically. 'Just goes to show some folk never learn. I guess I was too...'

Ellis never did learn exactly what it was Slim Cairns was about to say. The crack of rifle fire echoed around the narrowing valley, both horses shied, Slim Cairns crashed to the ground and Ellis managed to leap from his horse and take cover behind a rock. A second shot ricocheted close to his face, sending blinding dust into his eyes.

He peered over the top of the rock, his eyes reddened and painful and was just in time to see a figure running between rocks. He raised his gun, took a blurred aim and fired, but it was obvious that his shot had been well wide of its target. The figure crouched behind another large rock and returned fire, once again ricocheting close to Ellis's face. Ellis ducked down and rubbed at his reddened eyes. It was painfully obvious that whoever had attacked them was no stranger to the use of a handgun.

'Just what the hell do you think you're doin'!' called Ellis. 'I hope you know who I am.'

The reply came in the form of two shots, this time from a slightly different direction, and both thudded into the dirt close to Ellis's legs. This left him with the distinct impression that the assailant knew exactly who he was and was also quite capable of killing him at any time he chose. He curled himself up, almost into a ball, behind the rock as though this would in some way protect him.

Suddenly, he was aware that everything had gone strangely quiet although for a few moments he did not show his head. After about five minutes, the sound of a horse being ridden swiftly away made him stand and look.

His eyes were still watering from the effects of dust, but he was just able to make out a figure on horseback retreating in the general direction of Goose Rapids. Apart from an impression of the overall size of the assailant, which could have fitted a great many of the residents of Goose Rapids, Ellis had no clue as to the identity of the man. He watched horse and rider disappear from view for a few moments and then, wiping his streaming eyes, he remembered Slim Cairns...

Cairns was dead, obviously and bloodily so. The wound in the side of his head was large and very deep, too large and deep to have been inflicted by either a handgun or any normal rifle. In fact he had only ever seen an injury anything like it once before and that had been inflicted by a buffalo rifle.

A buffalo rifle was a large, unwieldy weapon, usually muzzle loading with single shot, especially designed to despatch those huge beasts quickly and efficiently, but it was well known that if used in very close range against a man, they were more than capable of removing his head.

He thought about the figure riding away and was quite certain that he had not been carrying such a weapon. Its long barrel would have been obvious. He started to search and discovered the weapon crudely hidden between two rocks, from where, he surmised, it had also been fired. He picked up the rifle, examined it for any clue as to the identity of the owner but could find nothing and then gathered his and Slim Cairns' horses which had scattered during the shooting.

SIX

'Nothin' wrong with your eyes,' pronounced Doc Freeman after he had examined the marshal. 'All they need is a good wash out, looks like you tried to shovel the whole desert in them.'

'I didn't shovel nothin',' grunted Ellis, 'A bullet came a bit too close for comfort, that's all.' He wiped his still painful eyes with a damp cloth and sat up. 'You sure there's nothin' else wrong?' he questioned. 'It sure feels like there's a couple of boulders still in there.'

'I've removed everything I can find,' replied the doc, firmly. 'Of course they'll be pretty sore for a time, there's a bit of bruisin' and a couple of minute scratches. Eyes are very sensitive, somethin' you can hardly see will usually feel like a rock. Just bathe them, that's all. They should be fine in another twenty-four hours.'

'Thanks, Doc,' said Ellis. 'It's a pity you couldn't do anythin' for Cairns.'

'Some hole!' Doc Freeman whistled softly. 'First time I've ever seen the effects of a buffalo rifle.'

Ellis rubbed at his eyes again and picked up the rifle standing nearby. He tested its weight in his hands and tried raising it to his shoulder, which was almost impossible.

'They usually come with a stand,' he explained. 'I didn't find a stand with this one, it had been rested between two rocks.' He attempted to raise the gun to his shoulder again but failed. 'These things pack a mighty punch an' could give anyone not used to 'em a mighty sore shoulder. I don't suppose you've had to treat anyone for a sprained shoulder, Doc?'

Doc Freeman shook his head. 'Not yet, if I do I'll let you know.'

'Do that,' nodded Ellis. 'Now I've been thinkin' that these kind of guns can't be too common these days. You must've been inside most folk's houses in your time, Doc, how many guns like this have you seen?'

Doc Freeman shook his head. 'Son, I don't go round lookin' for things like that. I couldn't tell you who has what.'

It was Hal Gibson who provided the information. 'They're more common than you might think, Mr Stack,' he said. 'This used to be buffalo country until the ranchers moved cows in. The last buffalo was shot in these parts maybe ten years ago. In them days almost every homestead had a buffalo rifle an' they all knew how to handle one. I've even fired one a few times myself, my pa has one. You're right about one thing though, if you ain't holdin' it right it sure can pack one hell of a painful kick.'

Ellis felt distinctly deflated. He had hoped that such a weapon would be unusual enough to pinpoint a possible assailant.

'How many do you think there are?' he asked.

'Oh...' said Hal, thoughtfully. 'Off hand I could name six but I reckon there's at least twice that many. Mostly they're stuck in some store-room or attic left to rust away.'

'Can you find out who is the owner of this particular one?'

'Only way I can do that is to hawk it round an' see if anyone admits to it,' said Hal. 'It ain't likely that whoever did own it is goin' to own up though, unless it was stolen. Still, if that's what you want, I'll try.'

Discovering the identity of the owner of the buffalo rifle proved a lot easier than Hal Gibson had predicted, although knowing the identity did not help Ellis at all.

It was quickly established that the rifle had been stolen from the Cattlemen's Association office where it had been kept on display and had been donated by a now long dead president of the association.

Although no one person had been identified, the information did help in some small way in that it meant that whoever stole the rifle had access to the Cattlemen's Association offices. Ellis asked Hal to draw up a list of those citizens with access.

Caroline Gray took the news of the death of her lover with apparent stoicism, although Ellis could sense that inside she was deeply hurt and shocked. Questioned as to whether or not she had told anyone that Ellis had intended to make the trip to Symmington Valley and urged, yet again, to think hard about having mentioned Slim Cairns being there to anyone else, she was adamant. Not a word had passed her lips except to Ellis himself.

So certain was she that she had not told anyone, that Ellis had to question himself. Had he dropped even the merest hint? He too was quite convinced that he had not. The fact remained, however, that someone had known, and they had known enough to take the buffalo rifle to ensure that Slim Cairns, or possibly himself, would be killed outright.

Ellis did not think that it was he who had been the primary target, which meant that whoever it was was capable of being named by Cairns. For several hours Ellis and his pencil worked hard, writing down names and drawing lines of possible connection between those names. In the end his pieces of paper looked like the plans for a spider's web.

The addition of the names of people with access to the Cattlemen's Association offices did nothing to improve the matter. Several names appeared on both Ellis's lists and on the list supplied by Hal Gibson, although there were three surprises.

On the list of those with regular access to the offices were Des Seely, owner of the hardware store, Mayor Thomas O'Hara and Mrs O'Hara. Of the three, Mrs O'Hara's name was the most surprising, although, as it transpired, it was she who actually owned the building.

In recent years, the Cattlemen's Association offices had become little more than a meeting house, a place to socialize occasionally, due mainly to the fact that there were now only two effective cattle ranchers in the territory, William Gray and Sam Paxton. There were a couple of smaller ranchers, but they controlled less than a quarter of the head count that either of the other two had.

Enquiries showed that Des Seely had once qualified for membership of the organization by virtue of owning a small ranch in his younger days, which he had sold out to Sam

Paxton. Ellis assumed that the mayor and his wife qualified by virtue of his being mayor or by virtue of the fact that Mrs O'Hara owned the place.

The Cattlemen's Association! The thought suddenly hit Ellis that either this association or the building seemed to be the one common thread between the murder of Sheriff Dan Robbins and the attack on him and Slim Cairns. Finding anything more common than the fact that the buffalo rifle had been stolen from there and the fact that Dan Robbins was murdered outside the back door of the offices proved very inconclusive and could only really be attributed to chance.

Despite the lack of any real proof, Ellis was firmly convinced that there was a connection and that he could narrow the list of suspects considerably by concentrating on the names which appeared on the list of membership of the Cattlemen's Association. Moreover, he felt that he might just force somebody's hand by making it known that he was concentrating on that body.

Of all the people who could have ambushed him and Slim Cairns, the only one who could most definitely be ruled out, male or female, was Caroline Gray, and only then because even she could not have disguised her size.

'It seems strange that a woman should be a member of the Cattlemen's Association,' Ellis said to Mrs O'Hara as he talked to her in the opulence of her home. He had decided to interview her there and not in the sheriffs office because he felt that she would be less guarded in her replies on her own, safe territory. 'I have known other women be members of such associations, but that was always because they also happened to own either cattle or a ranch.'

'And how do you know I don't own a ranch?' she smiled.

'Do you?' he asked, although he had taken pains to ensure that she did not.

'As good as,' she smiled disarmingly, a

smile which would have charmed most men. To Ellis however, her smile, apparent charm and seeming easy-going nature were about as trustworthy as a sleeping rattlesnake, safe while it was asleep but deadly when roused.

'Which means?' probed Ellis.

'Which means what it says,' she laughed. 'I am a wealthy woman in my own right, Mr Stack. You have probably discovered that apart from owning most of Goose Rapids, I also have considerable holdings and interests in other parts of the state.'

Actually this information was completely new to Ellis, he had simply not thought about anything like that. Even armed with this knowledge he did not think that it had any bearing whatsoever on the matter in hand.

'As a member of the association, you must have known about the buffalo rifle,' he said.

'I seem to remember some old rifle on one of the walls,' she confirmed. 'As to what it was or its significance I had absolutely no idea.'

'But you could have removed it.'

'As could any number of people, Mr Stack,' she pointed out. 'Tell me, just where is all this questioning leading?'

'Just trying to establish who killed Dan Robbins,' he sighed.

'And you suspect me?'

'At this moment I suspect everybody,' he said. 'But I do believe that the murderer was also a member of the Cattlemen's Association.'

She laughed. 'I suppose that limits the suspects to about ten or eleven.'

'A slight improvement on three or four hundred,' he smiled. 'Maybe when I find Slim Cairns' diary I'll have all the answers...'

'Cairns kept a diary!' she exclaimed. 'I didn't even know the man could read or write.'

'All I know is what I've been told,' smiled Ellis. 'Frank Heggerty maintains Cairns kept a book with names, dates and places. Not exactly a diary, but I believe it does contain the name of the killer.'

'Surely that was Cairns?' she said, seeming a little uneasy.

'I don't think so,' said Ellis, 'although I do believe he knew something and that something was enough for someone to kill him.'

She smiled disarmingly. 'Of course, why else should anyone want to murder him. I would say it is obvious, find the man who stole the buffalo rifle and you've found the killer of both Dan Robbins and Cairns.'

'Obvious but proving to be most difficult,' nodded Ellis. 'That's why I need to find this diary or book that Cairns kept. Well, once again, I thank you for your co-operation, Mrs O'Hara.' He rose and went to the door. 'Oh, and please, don't tell anyone else about the diary, there's no knowing just what the murderer might do if he found out.'

'No word shall pass my lips,' promised Mrs O'Hara. 'I wish you the best of luck, Mr Stack.'

Ellis was more than pleased with his talk with Mrs O'Hara, his prime objective had been achieved in letting it be known that a diary was in existence which, as far as he knew, it most definitely was not.

The idea had come to him as a means of forcing some action and in this he had secured the co-operation of Frank Heggerty and Jos McKay. They had agreed, on a promise from Ellis that he would intercede with the judge on their behalf, that they would let it be known to anyone who asked, that Slim Cairns kept such a diary.

During the day the first sign that Mrs O'Hara had told someone appeared in the sheriffs office in the form of the mayor, Mr O'Hara. His stated reason for visiting the jail was to check, in his capacity of mayor, that the prisoners were being well treated. It was confirmed by Heggerty and McKay that the mayor had casually mentioned the possibility of a diary. Both men played their part and the mayor left convinced that such a diary was in existence.

In the meantime, Ellis interviewed all the other members of the Cattlemen's Association and was received with reactions varying from what seemed genuine co-operation to downright hostility, the latter coming from William and James Gray and to a lesser extent from Caroline Gray.

Hal Gibson had been despatched to Symmington Valley with instructions to keep the caves where Slim Cairns had hidden under observation just in case anyone decided to search them in the hope of finding the diary. He was not to intervene, simply wait and watch.

The young sheriff waited and watched and was able to report back to Ellis later that evening that three people had searched the caves, which was two more than Ellis had expected. The first had been, not surprisingly, Thomas O'Hara, the mayor. The second had been Sam Paxton, which was a bit more surprising but the third and last had been the most unexpected in the form of Des Seely, the owner of the hardware store.

'Why Sam Paxton and Des Seely?' mused Ellis. 'Do you know of any connection between them?'

'Slim Cairns did work for Sam Paxton,' said Hal. 'It could be that he knew somethin' about his boss that Paxton didn't want makin' public.'

'Like what?'

'If I knew that, Mr Stack,' smiled Hal, 'it wouldn't be no secret would it?'

Ellis nodded. 'And Seely, where does he fit in with all this? What possible connection could there be between the owner of a hardware store, a rancher and the mayor and his wife?'

'Does seem strange,' admitted Hal, 'but I suppose there must be somethin'. Why else would he go out to the caves?'

'Why indeed?' sighed Ellis.

'You could always ask him,' said Hal. 'There ain't no denyin' that he was out there.'

'I probably shall do just that,' said Ellis,

'but not yet. I want one of them to make the next move.' He sighed and lolled back in his chair. 'Don't let anyone ever tell you bein' a lawman is easy. This case just becomes more an' more complicated. It'd make a pleasant change to have to face a bunch of outlaws where there was no doubt who was who and why.'

While the marshal was trying to make sense of the connection between Des Seely and Sam Paxton, those same two men, along with the mayor, Tom O'Hara, were meeting in urgent session. The meeting had been called by Sam Paxton and was taking place in the mayor's office. The venue had been chosen to make it appear that it was town business which was being discussed, even though Paxton was not a member of the town council.

'I'm not sure that we ought to be discussing anything,' protested the mayor. 'I don't know what it is you two have to talk about, but I fail to see how it can possibly concern me.'

Sam Paxton laughed. 'It concerns you, me an' Des,' asserted Paxton. 'It concerns you because I know it was you who took that damned rifle off the wall...'

'Only to clean it!' protested O'Hara.

'Very convenient!' sneered Paxton. 'The bloody thing's been hangin' there for years without anyone touchin' it. Why the hell should you want to clean it now?'

'Well if you're so sure it was me who killed Cairns, why don't you tell Stack?'

'Did you?' asked Seely.

'No, that's just it, I had nothin' to do with it. Sure, I took the gun home, but it was just like I said, I gave it a good cleaning. That was my wife's idea, she said it looked a mess stuck up on the wall.'

'Did you take the powder and shot?' asked Paxton. 'That was missin' too.'

'I had no need to,' said the mayor. 'Anyhow, why should I want to kill a man like Slim Cairns?'

Des Seely laughed. 'That's easy, Tom. We

all know that when it comes down to who's in charge in your house, or this town for that matter, it sure ain't you. Your wife controls you and if she decides she wants somethin' then you ain't about to stop her...'

'Meanin' what, exactly?' demanded O'Hara.

'Meanin' that she'd taken a shine to Slim Cairns,' said Seely.

'Just like her an' Dan Robbins were havin' it away regularly,' said Paxton. 'Oh, don't get worried on that score, Tom, there's no more'n a handful of us know about that.'

'I ... I knew about her and Robbins,' confessed the mayor. 'I even told Stack that I knew.'

The other two looked at each other in surprise. 'You told Stack?' queried Paxton. 'That was either very clever of you or very stupid.'

'Neither,' admitted O'Hara. 'Actually it was Stack who told me, all I did was admit I knew.'

'So he knows about your wife and

Robbins,' said Seely. 'If he found out about the rifle....' He drew a finger across his throat.

'OK, OK!' muttered O'Hara. 'So it looks pretty bad for me, the only thing is I didn't kill either of them.'

'I'm not so certain a jury would see it quite like that,' said Paxton.

'But it's the truth!' protested O'Hara. He suddenly sat back in his chair and glared at the other two. 'So why are you two here and why this meeting? All you have to do is tell the marshal what you know and he'll have to arrest me.'

'But we don't want you arrested,' smiled Seely. 'We know you didn't kill Dan Robbins.'

'You do? How do you?' He stared at both again. 'You know I didn't do it because one of you did it! Yeh, that's it, one of you two killed Dan Robbins.'

Neither man appeared upset at the suggestion and Sam Paxton laughed. 'So who killed Slim Cairns? Neither of us is denyin' that one of us did kill Robbins, but neither of us had anythin' to do with shootin' Cairns.'

'Then who did and why?' asked O'Hara.

'Exactly the question that Marshal Stack must be asking!'

This statement was made by Mrs O'Hara as she stood by the door to the office. She laughed, tossed her head slightly and came into the office, closing the door behind her. 'I can assure you, gentlemen, that my dear husband is quite incapable of killing anything, let alone another human-being.'

'Wh ... where ... were you listening?' demanded O'Hara.

'Of course,' smiled Mrs O'Hara, casually. 'What's more I've known all along who murdered Dan. What I wasn't sure of was why but I've been doing a little checking and thinking.'

Sam Paxton lounged back in his chair and smiled. 'I've got to hand it to you, you're one hell of a clever woman, probably too damned clever. So which of us murdered Dan and why?'

'The why is what had me foxed for a long time,' smiled Mrs O'Hara, taking a seat. 'The who came to me quite suddenly. At first I thought it was James Gray, after all I did see him over the body in the alley, but he swore that he had found the body and I believed him. Then I remembered that someone else had been in the alley just before James Gray.'

'And where were you?' asked Paxton.

Mrs O'Hara laughed. 'You were right about one thing, Sam, I had taken a shine, as you put it, to Slim Cairns. He had this thing about me lookin' exactly like his mother. All I can say is I hope he didn't do things to her like he did to me.'

'You're disgustin',' growled her husband. 'He was young enough to be your son.'

'Just like that dance-hall girl was young enough to be your daughter,' laughed Mrs O'Hara. 'Oh, I knew about her and one or two other indiscretions, but we're not here to discuss the morals of the O'Hara family.' She leaned on the table around which they were all sitting and looked smilingly at each man in turn, finally returning her gaze to Des Seely. 'I know you murdered Dan Robbins, Des, what I didn't know was why, there was no logical reason.'

'You saw me do it?' asked Seely.

'No, I didn't actually see you stab him,' she smiled. 'What I did see was you follow me and Slim into the alley. I had a key to the back door, that's where we went to er ... enjoy ourselves, Slim and me. You were waiting for us to come out again and I do believe that it was your intention to kill us both...'

'Kill you?' interrupted her husband. 'Why the hell should Des want to kill you?'

'Yes,' smiled Mrs O'Hara. 'Once I'd figured out that it was me who was the intended victim, the rest was easy. It just happened that Dan Robbins came along and you panicked. I'd say he saw the knife in your hand, asked what the hell you were doing and you panicked, Des. You ended up killing the wrong person.'

'And why would I want to kill you?' asked Seely.

'Don't be stupid, Des,' she laughed. 'I was foreclosing on that loan, remember? I was breaking you, taking every penny you had.'

'Just like you intended to do to me,' said Paxton.

'Just like I intended to do to you,' laughed Mrs O'Hara. 'To be perfectly honest, Sam, I hadn't tied you in with any of this but my guess now is that you and Des planned the whole thing together. It might have worked too had it not been for Dan Robbins.'

'Planned what?' asked Paxton.

She smiled and sat back staring at the three men. 'You and Des, Sam, you were both in danger of being wiped out so you agreed that I had to be killed before I could foreclose. I've got news for you, it wouldn't've made any difference, procedures are already underway. I don't know how you decided who was going to do it, but I guess you, Des, drew the short straw. You knew that I was meeting Slim that night and where. You followed us into the alley where you were to wait for us to come out. I was to be stabbed and I should imagine that Slim was to be shot dead and then you would claim that you killed him trying to defend me. All very simple, except for the fact that Dan came along to ruin everything.'

Sam Paxton laughed and slapped the table. 'I always did say you were a devious, schemin' woman. Sure, you've got it just about right, 'ceptin' that it was me who was to shoot Cairns as he ran out of the alley. Like you say, Dan came along, Des panicked and that was the end of that.'

'You didn't see me at the door, did you?' smiled Mrs O'Hara. 'It was only a couple of seconds after you'd gone that young James Gray appeared. He was the worse for drink, but I think the sight of Dan's body sobered him up. I was in the doorway, but I don't think he saw me, in fact I know he didn't.'

'And what about Cairns?' wailed the

mayor. 'Who the hell killed Cairns and why?'

'I think that was you, Sam,' smiled Mrs O'Hara. 'Slim was looking out of the window at the front, I believe he saw the two of you run away and tried to blackmail you.'

'You'll never be able to prove it,' smiled Paxton. 'Sure, that's what happened. Cairns saw what he thought was an easy chance to make a lot of money. I went along with it for a time but when Marshal Stack came on the scene I got worried. I didn't want him arrestin' Cairns because I knew he'd make him talk. I persuaded him to go to the caves and wait. I hadn't even thought about killin' him at that point, I just wanted him out of the way.'

'Then you found out that Stack knew where he was,' smiled Mrs O'Hara. 'You panicked too and killed Cairns. The buffalo gun was ideal. I'd said to Tom that it needed a damned good clean and he was stupid enough to bring it home. You stole it from our house.'

'Only thing wrong with that was that I

didn't know Stack knew where he was,' said Paxton. 'I saw it as a chance to throw suspicion on to someone else, Tom actually. It just happened that Stack turned up. He didn't see me and when he talked Cairns into giving himself up I decided that I had to kill Cairns.'

'Why didn't you shoot Stack while you were at it?' asked Mrs O'Hara.

'Too risky,' admitted Paxton. 'I probably could have done but I didn't want to chance anything going wrong. He didn't see me, I'm sure of that else he'd've had me in jail by now.'

'What about this diary Cairns had?' asked the mayor.

Mrs O'Hara laughed. 'What diary? There was no diary, no nothin'. That was just the marshal baiting a trap and you fell right into it. He told me hoping I would spread the word and I obliged by telling the three of you. That was partly for my own benefit, I wanted to see which of you two would make the first move since I wasn't certain of my facts even then. Only trouble is all three of you went to the caves. I know it threw me for a while and I think it's baffled the marshal too, but he isn't stupid, he'll soon have things worked out.'

'Me and Des, I can understand us lookin',' said Paxton, 'but why should you, Tom?'

Tom O'Hara looked a little bewildered. 'I'd got it fixed in my mind that it was my wife who'd murdered both Dan Robbins and Slim Cairns,' he said.

'Scared of losing your meal ticket,' smiled Seely.

The mayor ignored the remark. 'It looks like you two have just made another mistake,' he said. 'Des killed Dan Robbins and you, Sam, killed Slim Cairns. It appears that the both of us can claim to be perfectly innocent.'

'Not so,' grinned Paxton drawing a handgun and pulling a piece of paper from his pocket. 'I have here what is known as a confession, signed by both of you.' He showed them the signatures. 'Perfect matches, nobody could tell the difference. I've been copyin' them for a long time, gettin' them just right. I was going to shoot Tom right here in his office and then go round to your house and kill you.' He nodded at Mrs O'Hara. 'Since you're here, you might as well both commit suicide together. Don't you recognize the gun, Tom, it belongs to you?'

'Then why all that about me killing Dan and Cairns?' asked O'Hara.

'Just me bein' sadistic,' laughed Paxton. 'I just wanted to see what your reaction would be.'

Mrs O'Hara reached casually beneath her coat...

There were three shots; two, fired by Sam Paxton, found their targets, the first slamming into Tom O'Hara's chest and the second into Mrs O'Hara's head as she squeezed the trigger of the small derringer which appeared in her hand. The shot from her gun drew blood from Sam Paxton...

SEVEN

Sheriff Hal Gibson reached the entrance to the mayor's office just in time to see a lone rider heading off into the darkness, but he knew it would be a waste of time attempting to pursue him at that time of night. Apart from that, he was reasonably certain that he knew who the rider was anyway.

Hal bounded up the stairs and burst into the mayor's office where he found the mayor, Tom O'Hara slumped at an angle across his chair, mouth gaping wide, a thin trickle of blood oozing from the corner and eyes staring lifelessly. Crumpled on the floor, almost underneath the table, he discovered Mrs O'Hara, her usually blonde hair now stained deep red. However, a brief examination proved that she was still alive.

The sheriff looked about, somehow

sensing that there was someone else and he saw a figure cowering in a dark corner at the back of the room. Hal pointed his gun, which he had drawn as he had run to the office, and slowly approached the figure.

'Don't ... don't shoot!' pleaded Des Seely, 'I didn't do nothin', please, don't shoot.'

'Stand up, Mr Seely,' ordered Hal, still keeping his gun levelled at the store owner who falteringly obeyed. 'Sit down in that chair over there.' He indicated one of the chairs around the table. 'Toss any gun or knife you've got over here, then place your hands on the table where I can see 'em.'

At that moment Ellis Stack arrived and Hal nodded at the apparently lifeless body of Mrs O'Hara. Ellis moved the blood-sodden hair to one side, felt for a pulse on her wrist and proceeded to pull her from under the table and lay her flat on the floor.

'I'll go get Doc Freeman,' he announced. 'Can you handle it here?'

'Don't worry 'bout me, Mr Stack. It's her who needs seein' to first.

Doc Freeman lived about a hundred yards down a side street almost opposite the council office and when Ellis arrived, he was ready and waiting.

'I heard the shootin',' grinned the doc, 'so I just got my bag and waited. Shootin' usually means someone's been hurt.'

'Mrs O'Hara,' said Ellis. 'It looks messy, lots of blood, but I've seen worse. You'd best see to her though, you're the expert, not me.'

'Mrs O'Hara?' mused the doc, following Ellis out of the door. 'Has anyone told Tom?'

'I don't think he'll be that interested,' said Ellis. 'I only saw him briefly, but I'd say he's dead.'

'Bloody hell!' oathed the doc. 'Who...?'

'I don't know any details yet, Doc,' said Ellis. 'Hal Gibson is dealin' with all that, I just came for you.'

By the time Ellis and Doc Freeman reached the office, a crowd had gathered, all demanding answers to a babble of questions. Ellis ignored them all and guided Doc Freeman through and up the stairs.

Doc Freeman pronounced the mayor, Tom O'Hara, dead, shot through the heart. Mrs O'Hara had been very lucky, the bullet had done nothing more than gouge a slight groove in her skull. She recovered consciousness as the doc examined her, but he insisted that she was in no condition to be questioned. At her own insistence, Mrs O'Hara was taken to her own home where a maid was detailed to look after her.

Des Seely was only too ready to tell everything that he knew, in the greatest detail but conveniently forgetting to admit that it was he who had killed Dan Robbins. For the moment he laid the blame for that firmly at the door of Sam Paxton.

'Hal,' said Ellis, after Des Seely had been locked away for the night. 'By rights this is your business. If you want to go after Sam Paxton, that's your choice. I know I was called in to look into the murder of Sheriff

Robbins, but it looks like that's been solved.'

'But he's not been caught,' Hal pointed out. 'No, Mr Stack, this ain't my case, it's yours. Just tell me what to do.'

'For the moment there ain't that much you can do,' said Ellis. 'I'm goin' out to the Paxton ranch...' He raised his hand and smiled. 'I know, he won't be there or if he is he'll be ready for me. Don't worry, I'll be careful. I know damned well it isn't goin' to be any use goin' after him tonight, but I might just find out which direction he went.'

The Paxton household was ablaze with light from numerous oil lamps, most of which seemed unnecessary, but it did help Ellis to establish just who was in the house. Sam Paxton did not seem to be amongst them, but those who were there seemed very agitated.

The folk in the house were given ample warning of the approach of the marshal by the fierce barking of a large dog chained by the porch but for a time nobody inside the house made any attempt to come to the door. Eventually a tall figure did open the door, rifle held at the ready, and peered into the gloom. The dog continued barking and pulling on the chain and Ellis was glad of that chain, he knew the dog would have attacked had it been able.

'Who's there?' demanded the silhouette in the doorway.

'I reckon you must have a pretty good idea,' replied Ellis. 'Stack, Marshal Stack. I'm here to arrest Sam Paxton for the murder of Mayor Tom O'Hara and the attempted murder of Mrs O'Hara.'

'Well he ain't here!' responded the silhouette. 'We ain't seen him all night.'

'Pardon me if I don't believe you,' replied Ellis. 'It is an offence to harbour a known criminal.'

'Pa ain't no criminal,' snarled the figure. 'I'm Jeremiah, his eldest son. No sir, it ain't Pa who's the criminal, it's that damned O'Hara woman.'

'I'm not here to argue the rights and

wrongs of it,' said Ellis. 'That's lawyer's business. All I know is that your father has murdered Mr O'Hara and tried to murder Mrs O'Hara.'

'Tried to murder her?' queried Jeremiah. 'She's still alive then? More's the pity. Don't make no difference though, he ain't here. You're quite welcome to search if you want.'

Ellis knew that searching would be a pointless exercise but he nevertheless took up the offer if for no other reason than to establish his authority.

Inevitably nobody in the house or the bunkhouse had even seen Sam Paxton that evening and so could not say which way he went. However, there was one elderly hand who, whilst not admitting he had seen his boss, made the comment, unheard by the others, that if it was him on the run, he would head for the Talahoe Range.

'I went back to the mayor's office,' said Hal Gibson when Ellis returned. 'I found this.' He handed Ellis the small derringer pistol.

'It belongs to Mrs O'Hara; Des Seely says she pulled it on Sam Paxton and that he thinks Paxton was hit either in the arm or shoulder.'

'So we may have an injured quarry,' grinned Ellis. 'In the wild an injured beast is more often than not more dangerous for it.'

'Mr Stack,' said Hal, taking back the gun and slipping it into a drawer, 'if Mrs O'Hara did pull her gun first, wouldn't that mean that Sam Paxton could claim he was actin' in self-defence?'

'And Tom O'Hara?' asked Ellis.

'Unfortunate accident,' said Hal.

Ellis sighed and flopped into a chair. 'Hal, in circumstances like this it ain't the job of any lawman to decide if it was justifiable or not, that's for the lawyers to argue about, they get paid a damned sight better'n we do for it.'

'OK, if you say so, Mr Stack,' nodded Hal. 'Now you know I ain't too well read on the law an' since the mayor was the only lawyer we had in Goose Rapids, I want to know what I do about Des Seely.'

'Hold him until I say so,' smiled Ellis. 'He's admitted he's involved in the killing of Dan Robbins, that should be enough to hold him for a long while yet. You make sure you get Mrs O'Hara's statement first thing in the mornin'.'

Hal Gibson insisted on accompanying Ellis on his search for Sam Paxton, pointing out that Paxton knew the Talahoe Range very well, better than almost anyone else, but he, Hal Gibson, was probably the one man in Goose Rapids who knew the range at least as well if not better, since he had been brought up in the territory.

Phil Monks, the town blacksmith, was appointed acting deputy sheriff in the absence of either Hal or Ellis with instructions to look after the prisoners and to keep an eye on Mrs O'Hara. He was further instructed to inform the governor's office if neither of them had returned within seven days.

Having settled that and one or two other minor matters, Ellis and Hal started their journey to the Talahoe Range. However, they had hardly passed the last building in Goose Rapids when they were hailed by a lone and very harrassed looking rider.

'Marshal!' gasped the middle-aged man as he reined his horse to a halt in front of them. 'You gotta do somethin' an' quick, Sam Paxton's gone mad, he's taken my daughter, Mary, sayin' somethin' about holdin' her hostage.'

'Hold on, Mr Howard,' said Hal, attempting to calm the man down. 'You say Sam Paxton kidnapped Mary?'

'Ain't that just what I said,' grated Mr Howard. 'Sure, that's just what he's done. The man's suddenly gone mad. Who the hell knows what he'll do to her.'

'When was this?' asked Ellis.

'Last night, about ten,' panted Howard.

'An' what took you so long comin' to tell us?' Ellis asked again.

Howard slumped in his saddle and sighed

heavily. 'Me an' my wife were tied up, that's why! Hell, don't you think I would've been here sooner if I could. We were tied up an' it wasn't till this mornin' that my foreman found us. Him an' the boys are ridin' after Paxton right now.'

'A pity,' said Ellis. 'They could only cause more problems. How many of them?'

'Five,' replied Howard, 'an' I don't give a shit if it causes you problems or not just so long as I get Mary back. Somethin' must've happened to send Sam off like that.'

'He murdered Tom O'Hara,' said Hal. 'We're just off after him.'

Howard stared at Hal Gibson in total disbelief. Eventually he managed to speak. 'The mayor,' he gasped, 'he murdered the mayor? Why? Why the hell should he do somethin' like that?'

'There's no time to explain,' said Ellis. 'Right now it's far more important that we get your daughter back unharmed. Which way did he go when he left you?'

'How the hell should I know that?'

snapped Howard. 'I was tied up, remember?'

'You must have heard somethin', Mr Howard,' said Hal.

'Yeh, well, it sounded like he rode off towards the Talahoe Range,' muttered Howard.

'Don't worry, Mr Howard,' said Hal, 'we'll get her back OK.'

'Let's hope those men of yours haven't gone and done anythin' stupid,' said Ellis.

They left Howard staring at their backs, their progress now having an increased measure of urgency. Hal said it would take at least three hours to reach the mountains of the Talahoe range and once there, there were any number of ways Sam Paxton could have gone.

Hal did ask Ellis if it would have been better if they had raised a posse, but Ellis was not a great believer in the use of posses.

'Too hard to hide; you lose the element of surprise, especially against one man like this. They're fine if you're after a whole gang, but not much use otherwise. Besides, from my experience while most folk will suggest a posse, there ain't many of them same folk prepared to ride in one. They've all got good reasons why they can't just at the moment.'

'I guess you know best,' said Hal. 'Personally I ain't never had experience of a posse, Mr Robbins never had cause to raise one.'

'How old is this Mary Howard?' asked Ellis.

'About my age,' said Hal, 'maybe a couple of years younger.'

There was something in the way Hal Gibson spoke which made Ellis look at him and smile.

'I'd say you knew exactly how old she was,' Ellis grinned. 'I ain't been married so long as I don't know a thing or two. I'd say you and Mary Howard were kind of friendly.'

Hal gave the marshal a quick sideways glance and nodded slightly. 'I guess I've got a lot to learn, Mr Stack,' he said. 'That's the second time you've known somethin' just from a look or a word. Sure, it ain't no secret that me an' Mary was seein' each other regular like...' He blushed and lowered his head slightly. 'Nothin' improper mind, either her ma or pa were always around. Most times I saw her on a Sunday, after church.'

'Were there any plans to get married?' asked Ellis, teasing the young sheriff slightly.

'We'd talked about it,' admitted Hal, 'but nothin' too serious, I ain't in no position to take on the responsibility of a wife just yet.'

'You will be, very soon,' assured Ellis. 'They'll have to make you permanent sheriff after this.'

'I hope so, Mr Stack,' sighed Hal. 'There's a house with the job, that'd solve a whole heap of problems. Still...' He sat up straight. 'That's for the future, right now we've got to get her back safe.' He shot his superior a sharp glance. 'Don't you go worryin' none about me doin' my job right just 'cos of Mary.'

Ellis laughed. 'I'd say the least of my worries would be about you doin' your job right. How much further to the mountains?'

Hal gazed ahead at the distant hills. 'Two hours,' he said.

'Let's see if we can knock half an hour off that!' grinned Ellis.

In actual fact they trimmed the time by almost an hour and during their ride, Ellis had been on the lookout for likely ways that Sam Paxton might have taken. However, despite most of the journey being fairly flat grazing land, there were no obvious alternatives to reaching the mountains than the trail they were following.

The terrain changed abruptly, one minute flat the next rising quite sharply with bare boulders protruding through. From that moment onwards Ellis was on the lookout for any tell-tale signs left by their quarry.

It was Hal who spotted it first and Ellis

had to admit that he had missed it. Even when it was pointed out to him, Ellis had difficulty in seeing it, but suddenly it became quite clear and he wondered why he had not seen it.

A very faint trail led away from the main track, a trail apparently made by two horses, which made Ellis curse to himself for not checking if Mary Howard was on horseback or not. The only real sign was that the grass had been brushed backwards by the horses' hooves, but once pointed out it became more visible.

They followed this new trail for about half a mile before they came upon a clump of gorse bushes, amongst which they discovered the recent embers of a fire and signs that more than one person had been there. The embers were cold but plainly very recent and Ellis knew that they could not be more than six hours behind. However, looking ahead at the now towering rocky slopes of the Talahoe, he realized that six hours might as well be six days.

'Looks like they headed that way,' said Hal at first studying the ground and then pointing towards what looked like a sheer cliff of about two thousand feet. Seeing the look on Ellis's face he laughed. 'There's a narrow pass over to the right,' he explained, 'it ain't easy goin' but it's the only way through for more'n ten miles either way.'

'Where does it lead to?' asked Ellis. 'And why should anyone want to come this way, surely there are easier ways?'

'Easier, maybe,' said Hal, 'but certainly not quicker. Goin' this way the state border is about three days' ridin', pretty hard ridin' too, but goin' the main trail takes at least five days and there is far more chance of bein' seen and caught.'

'And once he's over the border my authority ceases,' said Ellis. 'There's talk about the territory joinin' the Union, but that's all it is so far. If he reaches the border, we've lost him.'

'I reckon he knows that as well as

anybody,' agreed Hal. 'What are we waitin' for, Mr Stack, let's go!'

Hal Gibson's description of there being a narrow pass was something of an understatement. There was indeed a narrow pass, so narrow that had a stranger such as Ellis chanced that way alone, he would have dismissed it as nothing but a deep, narrow fissure in an otherwise impenetrable wall of rock.

It was easy to see why this route had never been opened as a main trail; it was impossible for anything other than a horse to pass along. For the first mile they had to follow a shallow but fast flowing river, running between high walls of rock no more than five feet apart in most places. Hal told Ellis that at certain times of the year, either through being snowbound or flooded by melting snow, the route was completely impassable.

After the first mile, they found themselves still between towering walls but following a narrow ledge above the swirling water. The gully had now widened to about fifteen or twenty feet. Their progress was hampered by recent rock falls, but at each obstacle the fact that they were on the right trail was confirmed by the presence of very new scuff marks made by other horses passing that way.

'I think we're gainin' on them!' declared Hal, pointing at a hoof-print in some mud. 'It gets so damned wet up here that things like that either get washed away or filled with water. That one looks fresh.'

Ellis agreed. There was certainly more than enough water about in one form or another. Apart from the river, now some ten feet below them, the towering sides of the gully seemed to be permanently wet, a fact seemingly confirmed by the dense moss which covered almost everything. Fresh rock falls were easily distinguishable by their lack of moss and in quite a few places the moss had been disturbed by passing horses.

'How much more of this?' asked Ellis,

casting an apprehensive eye upwards. 'It could be that he's lyin' up somewhere waitin' for us. We wouldn't stand much of a chance.'

'We're safe enough for the moment,' laughed Hal. 'There's no way anyone could get up there and ambush us. How far? That's hard to say. I did this once in a day, but normally it takes about a day and a half. Distancewise, I doubt if we've covered more'n three miles since we started through the pass. Mind, three miles in this sort of country is a hell of a long way.'

'It's the same for Paxton,' said Ellis, 'maybe even worse since he's got an unwilling companion.'

Hal's face hardened slightly. 'Just so long as he's done nothin' to her!'

Ellis made no comment on that as they negotiated yet another obstacle.

'How long at this rate before we're through?' asked Ellis.

Hal Gibson looked about him and smiled. 'I'd say we've got a good chance of bein' through the worst by about sundown. We haven't been makin' bad time.'

As far as Ellis was concerned, their progress was painfully slow but since his guide appeared quite happy with it, he could not argue otherwise. Ellis also realized that people living in towns such as Goose Rapids and country dwellers in general had different concepts of time and distance from the city dweller.

Their slow progress continued for the remainder of the day and more than once Ellis could have taken an oath on the fact that they had passed the same spot several times. It was only the fact that he knew such a thing to be impossible which prevented him.

Looking up at the cloudless sky told Ellis little other than it had apparently become slightly darker during the course of the past hour and it was only by looking at his pocket watch that he knew it must be almost sunset.

During the past hour also, the gully had widened from about twenty feet to about forty and the sheer sides, once almost impossible to see the tops of, although still sheer, had lessened in height to about forty or fifty feet. Quite suddenly, as they rounded a steep, rock-strewn bend, they were out of the gully and out on to flat, inhospitable-looking, windy moorland with the peaks of two mountains soaring way above them. The only way through was along a wide, fairly gently sloping valley between the peaks.

Hal reined to halt alongside a small but quite deep pool of crystal-clear water.

'I ain't tellin' you your job, Mr Stack,' said the young sheriff, 'but I reckon we ought to bed up here for the night.'

'You're the man who knows where we are,' smiled Ellis, actually quite grateful to get his aching body out of the saddle. 'Right now it's you who's in charge. If you say we stay here, then we stay.'

'Best place,' grinned Hal. 'There's good

shelter over there...' He pointed to some overhanging rocks. 'Out of the wind which, believe me, gets mighty cold even at this time of year. We could go on a while, but it's more open and even more windy. Once we're over that rise...' – he pointed ahead towards the far end of the valley –'it's all downhill but for the first couple of miles just as hard as what we've just come through. After that it gets easier.'

'Anything must be easier,' grinned Ellis. 'I wonder how far ahead Sam Paxton is?'

'Not too far,' assured Hal. 'I saw some signs back there which I would say are no more'n a couple of hours old.'

'Who taught you to read the signs?' asked Ellis, quite impressed with his young companion. 'I can read 'em all right, but I could never tell how long ago they were made.'

Hal grinned as he looked about for firewood. 'I had me a good teacher, one of the best, an old Indian who used to work for my pa. That man could follow a fish through water if he had to.'

'I know the type,' nodded Ellis. 'They can almost smell a trail, just like a tracker dog.'

'Sam Paxton will be camped up somewhere not too far away,' assured Hal. 'With luck we should find him tomorrow. In the meantime I suggest we eat.'

Not having eaten all day, that was an idea with which Ellis wholeheartedly agreed.

EIGHT

'We never saw any sign of Howard's men,' observed Ellis. 'I thought he said they'd gone out after Paxton.'

Hal Gibson laughed. 'Meanin' no disrespect to Mr Howard's hands, but I'd say it was only a token gesture. Sure, they would've done somethin' had they found Sam Paxton, but they're nothin' more than ranch hands. As far as I know most of 'em don't even own guns. They're good cattle men though, some of the best.'

The sheriff and the marshal were sitting in the lea of a large, overhanging rock in front of a large fire. They had warmed up their meagre rations and were waiting for a pot of coffee to come to heat. Their bedrolls had been laid out, their horses unsaddled and left to graze on the ample but coarse grass and the saddles now acted as hard pillows.

'I wonder how far ahead Sam Paxton is?' mused Ellis. 'I think I'll go up ahead an' see what I can. You never know, he could be just over that ridge.'

'I wouldn't do that if I were you,' warned Hal. 'It's bad enough tryin' to pick your way in daylight. There's too many holes an' things to fall into an' break your leg or somethin'.'

Ellis looked up into the now black, starlit sky and nodded. 'Maybe you're right, but we make a start at first light.'

'First light,' agreed Hal, feeling the coffee pot and deciding that it was now hot enough to drink.

After they had finished their coffee, both men settled down for the night, Ellis realizing just how tired he really was.

Ellis awoke with a start and gazed up at the almost full moon which had appeared since he had bedded down. Something had woken him but he did not know what.

'You awake?' he hissed softly.

There was no reply and Ellis was somewhat reluctant to ask again and lay there staring at the moon and listening to the sounds of night high up in the mountains. He was rather surprised at just how many different sounds there were. He glanced across towards his companion and suddenly sat up.

'Where the hell are you?' he called. There was no reply and, in the dying light given off by the embers of the fire, Ellis could see that Hal's rifle, which had been alongside his bedroll, was also missing. He sat up, now fully awake and grasped his own rifle.

'Bloody young fool!'

Sensing that the young sheriff had done exactly what he had been warned against, Ellis nevertheless made a brief search of the immediate area just in case he was still around. Both horses were there which meant that Hal Gibson had gone on foot and as far as Ellis could see, there was only one direction he was likely to have gone.

At first Ellis almost ran, but after falling into two small holes, he decided that in one respect at least, Hal had been right, there were too many unseen hazards. However, he pressed forward, this time slowly and carefully and, after what seemed an eternity, he found himself looking over the ridge down on to a moonlit scene of grey and black rock. He stopped at the top of the ridge, looking and listening.

Suddenly, Ellis was aware of movement some twenty or so yards away and, although it was impossible to identify just who it was even in the bright moonlight, he knew that it could only be Hal Gibson. He sat and waited until the shadowy figure was almost past his position before he spoke.

'Bang! You're dead.'

The figure stopped and slowly turned to face the marshal. 'The only reason I didn't see you, Mr Stack, was 'cos I wasn't lookin' for you nor anyone else.'

'You must've been lookin' for someone,' said Ellis. 'I thought you said it wasn't a good idea to be out here alone at night.'

'It ain't,' insisted Hal. 'I almost fell down a big hole.' He came over to where the marshal was crouching and knelt alongside him. 'After you'd suggested it though, the more I thought about it the better I liked the idea, so I just took it into my head to go take a look.'

'And did you see anythin'?'

'I know where they are.'

Ellis was not too surprised. 'How far?' he asked.

'Maybe a mile,' said Hal. 'Holed up in a circle of rocks up against a cliff face. The only reason I didn't go in there an' then was 'cos there's only one way in as far as I could see and I didn't want to chance Mary gettin' hurt in the crossfire.'

'Very wise,' said Ellis. 'Is it possible to pass where they are without being seen?'

Hal thought for a moment. 'I reckon so, but only in the dark.'

Ellis laughed. 'Then you, my young friend, can saddle your horse and get yourself somewhere the other side of them.'

'Now?'

'Now!' said Ellis. 'You get yourself about a mile or so below them and just sit and wait.'

'How will I know when to do somethin'?'

'You'll know, I can assure you of that!'

'And what are you goin' to be doin'?'

'Pretendin' I'm a sheep dog,' Ellis laughed. 'I'll be drivin' them towards you.'

'Sounds like a good idea,' agreed Hal.

Ellis did manage a few more hours sleep but he was wide awake at least half an hour before the first dim signs of dawn appeared in the sky. He managed to revive a few embers of the fire and warm up what coffee was left in the pot before starting out.

The circle of rocks proved very easy to find and Ellis left his horse about a hundred yards away and ran between boulders until he was about twenty yards or so from them. Two horses grazed a little beyond the circle of rocks and there was definite movement, but Ellis was a little puzzled as to why anyone should still be there. He would have expected that Paxton would have moved out at or before dawn or at the very least be in the process of preparing to move out by this time.

Ellis moved closer and closer until eventually he was directly behind one of the large boulders which formed the circle. He peered over and saw a man crouched, back towards him, over a fire. He stood up and raised his rifle to his shoulder...

'Hold it right there!' At least that was what Ellis had intended to call out and he was not too certain if he had done so or not. As it was, he hardly felt the blow which ended his interest in the proceedings. Now, however, the effects of the blow were all too painful as he attempted to focus his eyes and his mind and struggle to his feet.

'Sorry 'bout your head!' Ellis groggily tried to locate the voice. 'I said sorry 'bout your head,' repeated the voice. This time Ellis thought he could tell which direction it came from. 'Wouldn't've happened if'n you hadn't crept up on us like that.'

The throbbing in Ellis's head grew more persistent and louder but his eyes began to clear and he eventually focused on something very large and seemingly covered in red hair. He recoiled slightly.

'Just 'cos you're wearin' that badge don't mean you got the right to creep up on folk like that,' said another mountain of hair, this time black, coming alongside the ginger-haired monster.

Ellis shook his head, which proved to be a mistake as it simply scrambled his brains again, but his eyes became properly focused and clearer.

'Who the hell are you?' he asked, at least that was what he thought he had asked but neither mountain of hair responded. 'I said, who the hell are you?' he repeated. This time the ginger hair moved and seemed to look hard at him.

'Don't reckon it matters none who the hell we are.' Ellis was satisfied that the words did come from the ginger hair. 'Thing is neither of us ain't done nothin' wrong, so why the hell should a marshal come creepin' up on us like that?'

'Because I thought you were someone else,' groaned Ellis, gently feeling his head and then looking at the blood sticking to his hand. 'I thought you were someone called Sam Paxton and a woman called Mary Howard.'

The two men looked at each other slightly bewildered for a moment and then burst out laughing.

'Hell, Jake,' laughed the black-haired mountain, 'I knowed you allus reckoned you was purtier'n me, but you sure don't look like no woman.'

'You neither,' laughed Ginger Jake. 'Mind, I almost forgot what a woman looks like it's been so long since I seen me one.'

'Yeh, I'll go along with that,' agreed the black hair. 'Must be about two months.'

Ginger Jake looked at Ellis and grinned. 'Nope, I don't think either Israel or me looks like no woman 'ceptin' maybe one of them Bigfoot women I hear about.'

'Bigfoot?' asked Ellis, his mind now beginning to regain something like its normal composure.

'That's what the Indians call 'em,' said Jake. 'We ain't never seen one ourselves an' we've been trappin' an' prospectin' all our lives. They say they is some kind of wild man what lives up in the mountains.'

Ellis had heard the stories but had never really thought about them and he certainly was not that interested now. 'The only wild man I want to see is one called Sam Paxton. He's got a young woman in tow. Have you seen either of them?'

'We sure ain't seen no woman,' said Israel, 'that's somethin' we both would've remembered. Your badge says you're a marshal, what's your name?'

'Stack, Ellis Stack,' replied Ellis.

The two men looked at each other again and nodded.

'Now that's a name we've both heard,' grinned Jake, stretching out his hand. 'Pleased to meet you, Marshal.'

One of the last things that Ellis wanted to do at that moment was risk his hand being crushed in the huge fingers that reached out to him but at the same time he did not want to offend. He gingerly offered his hand.

The sheer size of the man implied pure strength, but Ellis found himself pleasantly surprised at the gentleness of the man's grip. The same applied to Israel as he too insisted on shaking the marshal's hand.

'Hell, Marshal,' said Israel, apologizing again, 'I sure am sorry 'bout hittin' you like that but you'd be surprised just how many outlaws think we carry gold. I don't think I hurt you too bad though, it wasn't such a big rock an' I did throw it from maybe twenty feet.'

Ellis assured Israel that he had been hurt bad enough and enquired how long he had been unconscious.

'Oh, maybe ten minutes,' said Jake. 'Don't rightly know, time don't mean that much to us. Only time what matters is sundown an' sunrise. We been camped up here for three days now but we ain't seen no sign of anyone 'ceptin' you.'

'Unless they went through in the dark,' said Ellis, 'I would have thought it would have been impossible to miss them.'

'Could be 'cos we ain't been here all the time,' said Jake. 'We was out most of yesterday doin' some huntin'.' He nodded towards a nearby carcass which looked like a deer. 'Not much about 'ceptin' a few deer. I told Israel we was wastin' our time huntin' up here.'

'I wouldn't know anythin' about huntin' in

these parts,' said Ellis, gently feeling his scalp again and wincing slightly. 'Maybe I should apologize for creepin' up on you like that. These things happen though. Still, right now I've got me a murderer and a kidnapped woman to find, I'd best be on my way.'

'Murderer?' asked Israel. 'I only ever known one man who was a murderer before an' that was ... let me see ... why, it must've been more'n twenty years ago, feller named Flynn...'

'Nearer thirty years,' interrupted Jake. 'James Flynn, sure I remember him...'

'Gentlemen, if you don't mind,' sighed Ellis. 'I've got to be on my way. Sorry to have bothered you.' He pulled out his pocket watch and looked at it and then up at the sky. 'How long did you say I was unconscious?'

'About ten minutes,' said Jake.

Ellis looked at the watch again and sighed. That ten minutes had, in fact, been three hours.

Hal Gibson did not sleep very much that night; quite apart from the thought that his Mary was in danger, his two years as deputy sheriff had not really prepared him for anything like this. The chase was on and his adrenalin was running riot.

It had been only with a great deal of willpower that he had ridden past the camp. The thought that Mary was spending the night with Sam Paxton was almost too much for his strict moral upbringing even though he knew that there was nothing Mary could do about it. However, true to his promise to the marshal, he had ridden by and finally settled himself overlooking the trail about a mile further on.

The voices confused him; he could have sworn that one of them belonged to Mary but he knew that such a thing was impossible since he also knew that she and Sam Paxton were camped about a mile further back. The voice persisted, definitely coming from further down. Now it was joined by another voice which was quite unmistakably that of Sam Paxton. Hal looked in confusion back in the direction he had come and for a brief moment he hesitated...

'Hal!' The stifled gasp came from a young woman now standing in the small clearing where the young sheriff had slept the night.

'Mary!' gasped Hal, turning. Suddenly he was running towards her. 'Mary! thank God I've found you!' It seemed perfectly natural that they should end up in each other's arms.

'Very touching!' sneered a voice.

Hal pushed Mary away but realized that any attempt to draw his gun would prove fatal. The two men stared at each other for a few moments and then Sam Paxton laughed.

'I've got to hand it to you, young Hal,' he said. 'I didn't think you'd dare make a move without the marshal's say-so.'

Hal was about to say that the marshal was

not far behind, but decided against it.

'It's all right for him,' Hal said instead, 'all he has to do is post you as a wanted criminal an' then sit back and wait.'

'But you had to be the hero and ride out to rescue your woman,' sneered Paxton.

'I'd've done the same no matter who it was,' said Hal.

'Yes,' grinned Paxton, 'I do believe you would. Now, the question is what am I goin' to do about you? I suppose the marshal has posted me as wanted for murder, so it probably doesn't matter that much what I do.'

'You'll never get away,' warned Hal. 'Murderin' a sheriff is one thing every state backs every other state on.'

'But I haven't murdered you yet,' grinned Paxton.

'I meant Dan Robbins.'

Paxton shook his head and laughed. 'So that's it! I should've expected as much. Des Seely has told you I killed Dan Robbins. Sure, I was there, I'll admit that but it was

Des who knifed him, he just sort of panicked.'

'Actually I had it figured somethin' like that,' said Hal. 'The best thing you can do is come back an' clear your name.'

Paxton laughed again. 'But I did shoot Slim Cairns with the buffalo gun. No, sir, I think I'll take my chance on the run.'

'And run you will, Mr Paxton,' warned Hal. 'Now, I don't care what you do for the moment, but I'm not lettin' you take Mary any further...' He put his arm around her shoulder and started to lead her away. 'You'll get caught eventually an' I'm prepared to wait for that day. Right now the only way you'll stop me takin' Mary back with me is to shoot me.' He now had his back to Paxton...

'Hang on, Marshal!'

Ellis looked back to see Jake and Israel packing their belongings and saddling their horses. He was very surprised at the speed with which such large men moved and it took no more than five minutes before they were astride their horses and alongside him.

'We was about to pack up anyhow,' explained Israel. 'We just figured that maybe we could be of some use to you.'

'How?' asked Ellis.

'Look ahead, Marshal,' said Jake pointing. 'It's pretty open country just here but about four or five miles down it turns into thick forest. Now we ain't sayin' that you don't know your way round a forest, but we've lived out in the wilds almost all our lives so I reckon we is kinda more expert at it than you.'

Ellis looked ahead and could see that it did appear to be very thickly wooded.

'There's another thing too,' said Israel, 'some sort of tradin' post about ten miles on. Not exactly the sort of post we is used to, more a hideout for outlaws on the run, just like this Paxton feller you're after.'

'I could deal with it,' said Ellis.

'Marshal!' grinned Israel. 'We ain't talkin' 'bout no regular tradin' post. If they even suspect that you is a lawman you'll never get beyond the place alive an' believe me no man'd ever find your body.'

'I've been in places like that before,' said Ellis, 'and I'm still here to tell the tale.'

'OK, Marshal,' shrugged Israel, 'your business; don't say we didn't warn you.'

Ellis grinned. 'Thanks. OK, maybe you're right, maybe I could use you, especially if Paxton takes to the forest away from the regular trail.'

'Now you're talkin'!' grinned Israel.

For the next ten minutes Ellis had to endure an account about they had once been sworn in as deputy sheriffs, an account which Ellis was quite certain gathered embellishments whenever it was recounted which was probably not too often.

The one thing that had surprised Ellis was that there had been no sign of Hal Gibson. He realized that he had ordered the young sheriff to remain where he was until something happened, but since nothing had happened for more than three hours, he would have expected Hal to investigate.

He had not mentioned the fact that Hal Gibson was ahead to either of his new companions but Jake suddenly raised his hand and motioned them to stop. Very slowly, eyes darting everywhere, both men drew their rifles from the saddle holsters.

Ellis had not heard a thing above the constant babble of both men and he was more than surprised that either of them had heard or seen anything.

Without a word passing between them, both men slid silently from their saddles. Ellis was about to speak but Israel motioned him to keep quiet and to get off his horse.

That something unusual was afoot, Ellis had no doubts although he had heard and seen nothing. In such matters he was prepared to bow to the superior knowledge of others with more experience. All three stood motionless, hardly breathing, eyes darting and ears on the alert. Jake nodded to Israel and both men looked towards a thick patch of brush but still Ellis could not hear a thing.

Again without speaking, the two big men split up, going either side of the brush, leaving Ellis with the direct approach. He was not certain if he was intended to move or not, they seemed to have forgotten that he was there. He moved slowly forward wondering if what the men had really heard was something like a deer.

Suddenly, again without a word passing between them, the two big hunters raced into the brush and Ellis quickly followed. From the scene that greeted them, Ellis was never able to fathom out just how either man knew and they certainly never told him.

Hal Gibson lay spreadeagled on the ground, flies already buzzing busily around the blood now congealed around his right ear. Ellis rushed forward and examined the young sheriff and was satisfied that he was still alive.

'Looks like you know him,' observed Jake.

'Hal Gibson, Sheriff of Goose Rapids,' said Ellis. 'He's with me.'

Israel snorted. 'Damned funny way to act. If he's supposed to be with you, what's he doin' here with his skull split?'

'Yeh, damned peculiar,' added Jake. 'You're both together but you ain't an' both of you almost gets yourself killed.'

'It'd take too long to explain,' sighed Ellis. 'C'mon, help me get him cleaned up.'

'Leave him to us,' grinned Jake, 'we knows a thing or two 'bout cleanin' up wounds an' things. Learnt it from the Indians back up in Canada...'

Ellis closed his ears, allowed them to continue to attend the wound and went to look for Hal's horse.

NINE

By the time Ellis located Hal Gibson's horse, Jake and Israel had cleaned up the wound and applied a greenish paste which, they assured him, was another Indian remedy guaranteed to kill off any possible infection. Ellis had his doubts but did not question them.

'He's in a bad way,' announced Israel. 'That weren't no bullet, somebody hit him purty damned hard with either a rock or a rifle butt. There ain't no sign of a rock lyin' round so it looks like a rifle butt. Fine lawman he is, lettin' someone come up behind him like that.'

Ellis chose not to comment, but he tended to agree. 'How bad?' he asked.

'Let's just say that if'n he don't get to a doctor purty damned soon, this Goose

Rapids you was talkin' about is gonna need a new sheriff.'

'I thought that stuff you put on would cure anythin'?' said Ellis.

'So it will,' said Jake, 'It don't cure broken bones though an' it looks like his skull's broken.'

'Looks like you got a choice to make, Marshal,' said Israel, logically. 'If you don't get him back to a doctor he'll more'n like die but if you do, you can say goodbye to this Paxton feller an' the woman.'

Since becoming first a sheriff and then a US marshal, Ellis had had to make many difficult choices but none had been as difficult as this. On the one hand he could not allow Hal Gibson to die but on the other he had to at least try and save Mary Howard. He knew that Hal would have insisted that Mary must come first and in a sense that was where his duty lay. He mulled over the problem for a while and then looked hard at the two mountains of hair.

'Have you ever been to Goose Rapids?' he asked.

'Ain't never heard of it before,' said Jake. He too looked hard at Ellis and slowly shook his head. 'Marshal, I knows what you is thinkin'. You is thinkin' that me an' Israel could take the sheriff here back to this Goose Rapids...'

'I can't see any other way,' said Ellis.

'Meanin' no disrespect to either you or this young feller,' said Israel, 'but this ain't our problem, Marshal. Only way we've kept alive so long is by not gettin' involved in things that don't concern us.'

'But a man's life is at stake!' stressed Ellis. 'You can't just let him die.'

'Ain't no need for that,' said Jake. 'All you gotta do is take him back.'

'And leave the girl to God knows what fate!' said Ellis. 'You can't just turn your back on him.'

'Wouldn't be the first time,' said Israel. 'We had to leave two injured prospectors to a bunch of maraudin' Indians once even though we knew exactly what'd happen to 'em.'

'That was different,' pleaded Ellis. 'I can understand you doin' somethin' like that if your life was in danger, but there's no danger to you this time.'

Jake thought for a while. 'What's this Goose Rapids place like? We make most of our livin' huntin' an' trappin' an' sellin' furs. Is there any huntin' there? We heard it was nothin' but flat cattle ranges on the other side of this lot.'

'That's all it is,' Ellis was forced to admit. 'Look, I'll make it worth your while. I can guarantee you a hundred dollars apiece if you'll just get him back.'

'Hundred dollars!' said Israel, thoughtfully. 'I ain't seen me that much money in many a month.'

'Make it two hundred apiece,' said Jake.

Ellis inwardly sighed with relief, although he tried not to show it. 'All I can promise is a hundred,' he said, 'but it could be that we could come up with more.'

Jake was apparently the rather more hardheaded businessman than his partner.

'OK, supposin' we agrees an' supposin' we gets him back to this Goose Rapids all in one piece,' Jake said, slowly. 'In the meantime you goes after this woman. There ain't no guarantee that you ain't gonna get yourself killed. Where the hell does that leave us? We ain't got no guarantee you promised anythin'. All the folk in this town do is say thanks for bringin' our sheriff back, maybe give us a couple of bucks out of town funds an' order us out of town.'

'Can either of you read and write?' asked Ellis.

Both men shook their heads. 'Ain't never had no need for schoolin',' said Israel. 'We can count providin' the numbers don't get too big, but that's about all.'

'I can count up to a hundred real fine,' said Jake, 'an' in whole hundreds, it's the bits between that cause trouble, 'specially when it comes to tryin' to read numbers.'

'A pity,' said Ellis. 'Anyhow, all I can do is

give you a letter to the town council tellin' them to give you a hundred dollars apiece. That ought to guarantee your money.'

'Two hundred!' insisted Jake.

Ellis knew very well that he was on unsafe territory even guaranteeing the two trappers one hundred dollars and there was no way he could guarantee them one cent more.

'One hundred,' he repeated firmly. 'I'll make sure you get that much at least even if I have to pay it myself.'

The two men looked at each other for a moment or two and, without a word passing between them, they nodded briefly and Israel spoke.

'I guess you got yourself a deal, Marshal,' he sighed. 'Our trouble is we is too darned soft-hearted for our own good. Now, remember what we said about it bein' thick forest a few miles further on an' about the tradin' post. I ain't got no doubts you can handle them guns of yours but the kind of folk what can be found at this tradin' post ain't the kind to stand face to face an' fight.

A bullet in the back is their usual way of dealin' with folk.'

'I'll remember,' assured Ellis. 'I reckon Sam Paxton will keep to the trail since he isn't a woodsman either. Where he lives there's hardly any trees at all, just miles an' miles of cattle ranges.'

'There's just one more thing,' said Jake, leering slightly. 'If he does reach the post, it could be that he'll get himself killed just 'cos he's got himself a woman in tow. Even if he ain't killed, they is just as likely to take her off him an' pass her between whoever's there an' maybe even keep her for a while for any passin' drifter to make use of.'

'Then I'd better get there before they do,' grimaced Ellis. He found a piece of paper and hastily scribbled out instructions for the payment of one hundred dollars to each man, although he had the feeling that there would be a certain amount of haggling if not downright refusal to pay, but that was a chance he had to take.

'Good luck, Marshal,' grinned Jake, taking

the paper and stuffing it roughly into his shirt pocket. 'Don't you worry none 'bout the young feller here, he couldn't be in safer hands.'

Actually Ellis had the feeling that Hal Gibson was indeed in very safe hands.

He finally bade them both farewell and rode off, all the time looking for signs that Sam Paxton had left behind.

The four miles that Israel and Jake had said lay between them and the forest in actual fact turned out to be less than two miles but they had not exaggerated the density. The trail was, in some places, almost completely lost under dense vegetation and just as Ellis was beginning to think that he had strayed from it, it would suddenly appear again, if only briefly.

Signs that at least two horses had passed before him were all too plain in the form of broken twigs, branches pushed aside and the occasional hoofprint in soft ground. The fact that the trail was not very well worn testified to the fact that travellers were very rare. However, Ellis could fully understand why outlaws should want to come here and why such a thing as the trading post should exist. A man could probably hide out for as long as he chose and whoever had decided on opening the post had had a keen eye for business however dubious that business should be. He surmised that the post was probably run by an outlaw in any case.

Ellis had to assume that Sam Paxton and Mary Howard had already reached the trading post and he also had to assume that the worst had happened and Mary had been taken. He sighed sadly but knew that there was absolutely nothing he could do about it. As unpleasant as the experience might be for any woman, the one and only consolation he could draw was that he had never heard of any woman actually dying as a result of such an experience. As for Sam Paxton, he would have to wait, Ellis's first duty was to ensure that Mary Howard was returned to her family.

The trail was more marked than it had been for some time, although it had plainly not been used recently and this fact alone bothered Ellis. For at least a mile now he had not seen any obvious signs of anyone passing that way. He felt that somewhere he must have missed the signs and that they had branched off. He was just about to turn back and look more carefully when the sound of voices some distance ahead attracted his attention.

Israel and Jake had told him that the trading post was about ten miles, but having experienced the two trappers' idea of distance, he knew that he could easily discount that. It was equally possible that the post was just around the next bend or be another twenty miles. The sound of voices again wafted up on the quite strong wind and Ellis was inclined to the view that the trading post was in fact just around the next bend.

Ellis halted and examined the vegetation

and trees all around him for signs that Sam Paxton and Mary had passed that way and in fact he found himself looking at leaves and branches and almost convincing himself that they had been disturbed.

Eventually he decided that he was seeing things that were not there and made the decision to back-track to the last point where the signs had been unambiguous, which turned out to be rather further back than he had expected.

The signs ended at a small stream and it seemed perfectly logical that for some reason Sam Paxton had taken to the stream, although there were no obvious indications. Ellis followed the stream down for a few hundred yards and was met by a deep hole as the water suddenly cascaded for about 200 feet. An examination of the ground convinced Ellis that they had not gone that way.

Following the stream up for a couple of hundred yards seemed to indicate that Sam Paxton had not gone that way either, since that too ended at a high waterfall, this time at the foot of it. Somewhat mystified and rather regretting his own inabilities and limitations as a tracker, Ellis returned to the trail and followed it downhill again, this time travelling very slowly and stopping to examine every suspect mark, although none appeared to indicate the passage of horses. On two occasions he thought he had found something but even he was quickly able to establish that they were made by deer.

He found himself back at the point he had heard the voices and once again listened. This time, however, he heard nothing and rather reluctantly decided to move on and investigate.

The trail was suddenly squeezed between two towering cliffs, rising something like 500 feet and it seemed quite obvious that any traveller would have to go through this pass, which actually proved to be quite short, no more than a hundred yards. At the far end, situated amongst a mass of rocks, was the trading post.

There was no mistaking it, a large sign swung outside declaring it to be 'Harper's Pass Trading Post – Gold and skins bought, hardware and dry goods sold.' Opposite the main single-storey building were three other wooden shacks, all in need of repair of some sort. There was also a corral at the rear of the three shacks in which Ellis could see five horses at least.

He remembered the warning Jake and Israel had given that lawmen were far from welcome and his hand instinctively reached up and touched his badge of office. His fingers lingered over it for a moment before he unpinned it and slipped it into his pocket. He smiled ruefully and would have preferred to have left it where it could be seen, but he felt that discretion was possibly the safest course for the moment.

Ellis was forced to smile, if a little ruefully, as he slowly rode through the pass towards the trading post. It really didn't matter if he displayed his badge or not since, as seemed likely, Sam Paxton was there, one word from him would be sufficient.

His arrival seemed expected, which was no surprise since he must have been plainly visible as soon as he entered the short pass. Four men slowly emerged from the main building and lounged under the cover of the porch, thumbs casually hooked into gunbelts, a sign which Ellis knew only too well as being ready to draw and fire if necessary. He too casually checked that his own Colt was free and ready to draw. His other hand gripped his rifle. The four men on the porch and Ellis knew exactly what to expect and eyed each other malevolently.

'Don't get too many folk comin' from that way,' drawled a fifth man as he emerged from the trading post. He gave the appearance of being the owner, dressed reasonably neatly in what had once been a white apron but was now badly stained. 'Last time we had anyone through from there must've been more'n six months ago. You tradin' or just passin' through?'

'He don't look like no trapper nor

prospector,' announced the tallest of the other four men. 'I got me a nose for some things an' I don't like the smell he gives out.'

'You don't exactly smell like a bed of roses yourself,' countered Ellis. 'No, sir, I ain't here for tradin', I'm here to hide up a while.'

'Hide up from who?' demanded one of the others.

'US marshal,' grinned Ellis. 'Him an' me don't see eye to eye on a couple of things an' I get the idea that he'd like to settle things with a bullet.'

'US marshal?' queried the owner of the trading post. 'Only US marshal I know of in these parts is Marshal Stack.'

In a way, Ellis was somewhat flattered that his reputation had reached this outpost of civilization but he was wary.

'That's him,' confirmed Ellis. 'You know him?'

'Only by reputation,' replied the owner. 'What you done to have him on your tail?'

'He ain't on my tail,' said Ellis. 'I guess I'm about a week ahead of him. I killed a sheriff back in Goose Rapids, Dan Robbins.'

'I heard about that,' said the tall man. 'You killed him, how?'

Ellis smiled, it seemed obvious that the man was testing him. He drew his knife and played with it. 'In the heart,' he smiled. 'I prefer knifin' to shootin', attracts less attention.'

'Yeh,' grunted the tall man, 'that figures, I heard he was knifed. What's your name?'

Ellis had to take a chance. 'Cairns, they call me Slim, that'll do.'

The man nodded and appeared to relax a little. 'That adds up,' he said, addressing the owner. 'I knows Frank took off to work for some rancher out at Goose Rapids...'

'Frank Heggerty?' interrupted Ellis. 'You know Frank Heggerty?'

'Ought to,' grinned the man, 'seein' as how him an' me are brothers...' Ellis inwardly breathed a huge sigh of relief, he just almost used Frank Heggerty's name. 'Yeh, I heard he took up with two other fellers some time ago, name of Slim Cairns and Jos McKay. I saw McKay once, just before they went to Goose Rapids.' Once again Ellis blessed his choice of a name.

'Frank and Jos are both in the town jail,' he said, uncertain if the information was known or not. It appeared that it was.

'So I heard,' grunted Heggerty. 'I also heard that you'd disappeared. Nice to meet you, Slim.'

The tension suddenly disappeared and Ellis dismounted, tethered his horse to the hitching rail and followed the men inside the trading post. The interior was dark and very dusty and seemed cluttered with all manner of hardware and provisions, including a large pile of unsavoury smelling animal skins. The men pushed by the skins and went to the back of the store where there was a small counter behind which were displayed a surprisingly wide variety of drinks.

'We got beer if you want it,' announced the owner. 'Brewed it myself, better'n you'll taste even in the big towns.'

'Beer sounds fine,' agreed Ellis suddenly realizing that he was rather thirsty.

The beer cost twenty-five cents and, contrary to expectation, was indeed amongst the better brews he had tasted.

'If you want food you can either cook it yourself over in the bunkhouse...' –Ellis assumed that at least one of the tumbledown shacks must have been the bunkhouse –'or you can wait till tonight when I does the cookin'...'

'An' if you'll eat the shit he cooks you'll eat anythin'!' jibed one of the men.

The owner ignored the remark. 'I charge fifty cents a night for a bunk, an' that includes breakfast. Evenin' meal is extra, twenty-five cents, but like I say, you're free to cook your own if you want to.'

'Sounds fine to me,' grinned Ellis. 'I sure ain't no cook, I could even burn water.'

'Burnt water is better'n his cookin',' the man jibed again.

'Take no heed of Seth,' grunted Heggerty, 'he's only too ready to finish off other folk's leftovers no matter who cooks it.'

Seth grinned, displaying an array of blackened stumps of teeth. 'I've tasted worse,' he confessed. 'You got any spare cash, Slim?'

'Nope!' replied Ellis firmly, sensing that he would have to keep a wary eye open for thieving hands. 'I ain't got barely enough for my own needs.'

'Take no heed of Seth,' said Heggerty. 'He's allus beggin' off folk. Harper here though...' – he nodded at the owner –'he's the one to watch. If you buy anythin' off him I hope you can add up 'cos I'll guarantee he can't, leastways not in your favour. Everythin' allus seems to come to a dollar more'n it ought to.'

The names of the outlaws – as they turned out to be – were Henry Heggerty, Seth Chaplin, John O'Rourke and Sean Kelly. In his saddle-bags Ellis knew that he had posters on all four, although he seemed to remember that the total value of them all was no more than about $100. Harper, the trading-post owner who had also named the pass after himself, was an unknown quantity as far as Ellis was concerned. The only Harper he could remember had been a small-time gunman employed by a mining company and he had been short and fat, but surprisingly fast with a gun. This Harper was fairly tall, well built and named Tom.

'Is there any other way through?' Ellis asked since it was obvious that none of them had seen Sam Paxton. 'I sure couldn't see none.'

'That's 'cos there ain't none,' grinned Harper. 'No, sir, anyone headin' through the forest or them mountains has got to come my way, that's why I chose this place.'

'I wouldn't've thought it was worth your while,' said Ellis. 'You can't get that many folk through.'

'More'n you might think,' grinned Harper. 'There's a few trappers about an' I give 'em a fair price for their pelts. There's also a few prospectors but most of them only come for supplies now an' then. I buy some gold but not that much.'

'An' then there's folk like me who are on the run from the marshal,' said Ellis. 'It looks like you get a fair few of them too.'

Heggerty looked sharply at Ellis. 'What makes you say that? How'd you know we is hidin' from the law? None of us ain't said nothin'.'

Ellis hand slipped casually to his side ready to draw. 'I'm just guessin'. I was with your brother, remember. I know he talked about you more'n once an' it was plain you an' the law weren't the best of friends.'

Heggerty relaxed and ordered another beer. 'Guess so,' he said. 'Yeh, that's why we is all here. It's a bit of a hell-hole but I guess even this is better'n jail.'

Harper grinned. 'Folk like you keep me in business. No, sir, there ain't no way through other than the pass, not unless you can fly.' He laughed. 'Only other way through is about two hundred miles south.'

It seemed certain that Sam Paxton had deliberately held back and Ellis had missed him. All he could do for the moment was sit tight and wait if this was the only way through.

TEN

The wait proved to be rather longer than Ellis had expected. It had been about midday when he had arrived at the trading post and even allowing for Sam Paxton to have holed up somewhere and for whatever reason, he would have expected him to have arrived sometime during the afternoon.

It was also plain that Henry Heggerty still harboured suspicions about the man who called himself Slim Cairns and was in the habit of suddenly asking questions which he, Heggerty, supposed that only Slim Cairns would know the answers to. Ellis's replies were greatly helped by the fact that he had talked to both Frank Heggerty,

Henry's brother, and Jos McKay in some depth and had gleaned certain facts which would normally only be known to someone like Slim Cairns.

Despite the answers appearing to satisfy Henry Heggerty, Ellis still had the feeling that there was a great deal of suspicion there. However, providing he could keep the charade going long enough, at least until the arrival of Sam Paxton, he was not too worried. The arrival of Sam Paxton would, inevitably, bring the truth out into the open.

Darkness descended early, the last rays of the sun being shielded from the small valley by the towering mountains and as yet there had been no sign of Sam Paxton. Again, trying to sound casual, Ellis questioned Harper about the possibility of other routes through the mountains and once again he was assured that there were no other ways unless one could fly. The casual questioning of the four outlaws proved to be of little value since none of them really knew anything about the territory.

'Are you expectin' someone?' asked Henry Heggerty. 'You sure seem concerned about other ways through here.'

'Could be,' replied Ellis, 'but that ain't no concern of yours.'

The light had now almost disappeared and the moon had yet to rise and all six men were lounging about on the porch when a movement in the pass which, it seemed, only Ellis noticed at first, prompted him to leave the group and disappear into the darkness. The others did not take much notice since excursions either to the bunkhouse or to the ramshackle privy at the back of the store were quite commonplace. This time Ellis pressed himself against the wall of the store and listened.

'Well now, what have we here?' The voice was plainly that of Henry Heggerty. 'Hey, fellers, we got ourselves a woman.'

'Yeh!' croaked one of the others. 'A mighty good-lookin' woman at that.'

'Leave her alone,' came the voice of Sam Paxton. 'I need her to make sure I get through safe.'

'Now that ain't neighbourly at all,' laughed Heggerty. 'Out here the rule is we share what we've got an' you got yourself a woman. Now don't go tellin' me she's your daughter or anythin' like that 'cos we all know that ain't true.'

Ellis thought about breaking cover but he peered round the end of the building and saw that all four outlaws had their guns drawn. Now was not the time. The only light was provided by an oil lamp hanging in the porch and its dim light would make hitting any target very much a matter of luck, besides which they were far too close to Mary.

'An' why do you need her?' demanded Seth. 'Sounds to me like you took her as a hostage.'

'That's about it,' rasped Sam Paxton, giving Ellis the impression that he was in some sort of pain.

'A hostage against who?' demanded Seth again. It appeared that someone must have hit Paxton as he cried out in pain. 'Looks to me like you stopped a bullet an' it's goin' bad ways,' continued Seth. There was another cry from Sam Paxton. 'Now, I asked you who you were runnin' from.'

'Stack!' gasped Paxton. 'Marshal Ellis Stack, maybe you ain't heard of him.'

'Stack!' said Sean Kelly. 'Sure, we heard of him. Seems like everybody is runnin' away from him.'

'Everybody?' queried Paxton.

'Yeh, we got another visitor tryin' to outrun the marshal. Slim Cairns, have you heard of him?'

'Slim Cairns!' exclaimed Paxton. 'Impossible.'

'He's here OK,' laughed Heggerty. He called out loudly, 'Slim, looks like them folk you was expectin' is here.' He spoke to Paxton again. 'He seemed to be expectin' you. He was worried there was some other way through an' he'd missed you.'

'Mister,' grunted Paxton. 'I don't know who you are, but the one thing I do know for certain is that whoever this feller is, he can't be Slim Cairns.'

'What makes you so certain?' asked Heggerty. There was something about the voice which made Ellis realize that Heggerty was taking no chances and was even then probably creeping slowly to the end of the building.

'Because Slim Cairns is dead, I know, I killed him myself.'

'Then just who the hell have we got here callin' himself Cairns?' rasped Heggerty.

Ellis had worked his way along the rear of the building and, in an uncharacteristic blunder, realized that he had trapped himself between the store and the sheer wall of rock behind it. He knew that Henry Heggerty was working his way around one end and he was quite certain that at least one of the others would be doing the same from the opposite direction.

'In here!' whispered the voice of Tom Harper so close to Ellis's ear that he almost shot without thinking. A large hand grasped his arm and pulled him through the door. 'Down here!' Harper instructed again.

In the dim light Ellis could just make out the figure of Tom Harper holding open what appeared to be a trapdoor. He chose not to argue or to question the trading-post owner's motives and clambered into the hole, finding himself in some sort of cellar. The trapdoor closed quietly over his head and he could hear something being dragged across the floor.

A few minutes later he heard a door open over his head and someone shuffling about. Whoever it was called out that there was nobody in the room and the door closed again.

In the meantime Henry Heggerty had decided to question Sam Paxton a little more closely and apparently painfully. It seemed, for the time being at least, that interest in Mary Howard had waned somewhat.

The questioning must have been taking place almost directly over Ellis's head, or at least very close to where he was now imprisoned, which he felt was the case, however unwittingly. He did try to open the trapdoor but failed to even lift it. Tom Harper had made certain that he could not get out.

'OK, mister, what's your name?' demanded the lightly muffled voice of Heggerty above Ellis's head.

'Paxton, Sam Paxton...'

'Paxton?' grated Heggerty. 'Sam Paxton the rancher?'

'There's only one of me as far as I know,' winced Paxton.

'The name's Heggerty, Henry Heggerty, I think you know my brother, Frank.'

'Frank! Sure, I know Frank, I ought to, I hired him along with Slim Cairns and Jos McKay.'

'And where are they now?' demanded Heggerty.

'I told you, Cairns is dead, I killed him and the other two are still in jail as far as I know.'

'That much seems certain,' grunted Heggerty. 'What you kill Cairns for?'

'He was tryin' to blackmail me 'cos I was involved in the murder of Sheriff Dan Robbins.'

'Seems like everyone wants to take credit for that,' muttered Heggerty. 'So, whoever is out there ain't Slim Cairns. Who do you suppose he is, Mr Paxton.'

'The only man I can think of is Marshal Stack,' replied Paxton.

'I just got round to thinkin' that myself,' rasped Heggerty. 'Thing is, we had us one feller here tryin' to pretend he was someone else, pretty convincin' too, but then he would know a thing or two about Frank, Slim Cairns an' Jos McKay if he had 'em locked up wouldn't he? Mind, it could be that you know so much on account of you is pretendin' to be someone else. Maybe you is Marshal Ellis Stack an' the other one was really Slim Cairns.'

There was a sudden cry of pain from Paxton. 'I *am* Sam Paxton, ask her, she ought to know, she's one of my neighbours' daughter.'

'He's Mr Paxton all right,' came the whispered reply from Mary Howard. 'I don't know if he killed the sheriff and this Slim Cairns or not, but he says he did.'

'Not the sheriff,' rasped Paxton. 'I said I was involved, but it wasn't me what stabbed him.'

'Who killed this damned sheriff isn't important, he was doin' us all a favour,' hissed Heggerty. 'The thing is it seems likely that whoever is out there is Marshal Stack. We've all got prices on our heads so it looks like we is goin' to need a hostage too. I gotta admit that we did have other plans for you, little woman, an' maybe we still might have, but for the moment you is better employed as a hostage for our sakes. I'm just puzzled about one thing, though: if this marshal was behind you, how the hell did he get in front? I had me a ride up into the mountains a couple of days ago an' it don't seem easy to give anyone the slip.'

'He was getting worse,' said Mary, her voice sounding firm, 'he said he was shot by the mayor's wife back in Goose Rapids. That was after he'd killed the mayor and then I suppose he killed her, I don't know. Anyway, you can see that his shoulder is going bad ways, that really started yesterday morning. We were forced to pull off the trail and hide up while I did my best to clean it up. That was after he'd clubbed the sheriff. I don't know if he killed him or not.'

'Sheriff?' exclaimed Heggerty. 'What sheriff? Is the whole damned mountain alive with lawmen?'

'Hal Gibson,' explained Mary. 'He was deputy to Mr Robbins.'

'And he was following too?'

'He said he was alone,' grunted Paxton, 'but I knew he was lyin'. I knew Stack wouldn't've let him come after her alone. I hit him with my rifle butt, pretty damned hard I've got to admit, but the idea was to just hurt him so bad that Stack would have to give up the chase an' take him back to

Goose Rapids.'

'Seems like you hit him too hard!' muttered one of the others.

There was a heavy crash as something was slammed down hard and Heggerty produced a flow of colourful obscenities. Eventually he calmed down.

'Mr Rancher Paxton,' Heggerty finally grated, 'I been on the run from the law most of my life an' that's more years'n I can remember an' in all that time I only ever killed me one man an' that was a dirty saddletramp who tried to kill me. Nobody ever knew 'bout him but that's 'cos nobody gives a damn about men like that. You, a respectable rancher have killed more men in a few days than even the worst do in a lifetime, or near enough...' He gave a derisory laugh. 'Most folk call the likes of me scum. I reckon they got their priorities mixed up somewhere.'

'If that is the marshal out there,' said Paxton, 'it seems he don't trust you.'

Heggerty grumbled to himself for a while.

'I guess if it was a case of him or me I'd have to kill him.'

'That goes for me too,' said another voice. 'I just spent me three years in the Pen an' I don't intend to go back there. For his own sake Stack had better keep away, I'll take my chance an' kill him if need be.'

Heggerty apparently thumped the table and laughed. 'Anyhow, we got us a hostage to make sure he ain't no trouble, courtesy of Mr Paxton.'

There was laughter and agreement from the others followed by Mary Howard shouting at someone and what seemed to be a hard slap. This appeared to cause much amusement.

'What about me?' moaned Paxton.

'You can leave as soon as you like,' replied Heggerty. 'From here on in you is on your own. None of us give a damn if the marshal catches you or not, but you don't take her with you, she belongs to us now.'

A few inches below the feet of the outlaws, Marshal Ellis Stack climbed on to a box and put his back against the trapdoor, pushing upwards with all his strength. This time there was some movement, enough for Ellis to be satisfied that he would be able to escape the cellar. For the moment he was quite content to await his chance at some time during the early hours of the morning. It had sounded as though the men above were engaged in some heavy drinking and he knew that things would be that much easier if the men were the worse for drink.

He had never realized just how slowly time could pass, but Ellis would have taken wagers on his time in the cellar being in excess of six hours. As it was curiosity finally got the better of him and he struck a match to check the time on his pocket watch. He looked at the watch disbelievingly as it indicated that he had been there for just over three hours.

He was just about to put his back against the trapdoor once again when the door above opened and heavy steps thundered the short distance from the door, sending dust down which almost made Ellis sneeze, but he managed to prevent himself. The footsteps paused for a moment, grunted and dragged something across the floor and apparently sat down.

Ellis silently cursed and waited for a while, but it appeared that whoever was up there had no intention of moving. After about ten minutes Ellis gingerly placed his back against the trapdoor and pushed slowly upwards...

Ellis almost fell off the box he was standing on as the trapdoor opened without resistance and he had to stop it opening too far. He peered through the narrow gap, his gun held ready in the direction he knew the man to be, and saw a dark figure apparently sitting on a box, looking out of the tiny, dingy window.

The easiest and simplest thing to have done was to shoot, the man would stand no chance, but Ellis knew that that would have brought swift and possibly fatal retaliation. He studied the figure by the window for a few moments and suddenly had the feeling that the man was asleep. This seemed confirmed by the onset of slightly rasping regular breathing.

Very slowly, Ellis eased the trapdoor back until he felt it rest against something, which appeared to be a full sack, and then gently lifted himself out of the hole. Had the man woken at that moment he would probably have had Ellis at a disadvantage, but he slept on.

Once free of the hole, Ellis stepped forward, reversed his gun and brought the butt crashing down on the back of the man's head. He was forced to deliver two blows as the man struggled to his feet after the first. The second sent him into Ellis's outstretched arms and he eased him to the floor. He was about to retrieve his rifle from the cellar when he had the idea of putting the man, who was Sean Kelly, into the cellar. It had proved a secure prison for

Ellis, apart from the trapdoor, but that problem was easily solved by dragging the box and the heavy sack over it.

His immediate priority was to locate Mary Howard and the most logical place to look was in the bar area of the store. That was where the stove was and the general focal point. It was also probably the most easily defended area.

Opening the adjoining door fractionally, Ellis peered through into the dimly lit store and smiled with a certain amount of smug satisfaction at being right, at least as far as Mary was concerned. He could just see her, apparently asleep in a chair but, although he could not see anyone else, he doubted very much if she was alone. Stepping silently into the store amongst sacks and boxes he was able to make out the figure of Tom Harper who also appeared to be asleep. Ellis crept forward and eased himself into position behind the trading-post owner and pressed the barrel of his Colt against the man's temple.

Eyes flickered but hardly a muscle moved. 'I heard you comin',' whispered Harper. 'I didn't think you'd be able to get out with the Irishman in there.'

Mary Howard's eyes flickered and she awoke with a start, almost crying out. Ellis raised a finger to his lips to tell her to be quiet.

'He's in the cellar nursin' a sore head,' whispered Ellis. 'Where are the others?'

'Don't know for certain,' responded Harper, breathing a slight sigh of relief as Ellis removed the gun from his head. 'One of 'em is overlookin' the corral, that's all I know for sure.'

'Have you got a gun handy?' Ellis asked.

'Right here,' said Harper, raising his hand to reveal an ancient but efficient Adams. Ellis instinctively levelled his Colt at Harper who smiled and laid the gun down. 'I don't reckon on usin' it either on you or them,' he continued. 'The best thing you can do is lock me in the cellar along with Kelly. I got my future to think about an' my life wouldn't be worth a cent if it gets out that I helped you.'

'I'll go along with that,' agreed Ellis. 'OK, the cellar it is.'

Mary Howard seemed totally bewildered at the turn of events, but she remained silent and huddled in the large chair, staring at the two men with a mixture of terror and wonderment.

Ellis followed Harper into the back room where both moved the box and sack. Ellis lifted the trapdoor and Harper sat himself on the edge prior to jumping down. He did not see the butt of Ellis's gun descending.

'Just to make it look right,' grunted Ellis, closing the trapdoor and pulling the box and sack back into position.

Returning to the main store, Ellis peered through a small, grimy window and could see two figures almost directly opposite. He was reasonably certain that one of them was Henry Heggerty but both men seemed completely unaware of what had happened inside.

Had he been on his own, Ellis had little doubt that he could have coped with the situation, but with Mary Howard being his main priority, he knew his limitations. He decided that a little bargaining was in order.

'Heggerty!' Ellis called out. 'Kelly and Harper are both out of action, not dead but they've both got pretty sore heads...'

Both Heggerty and the man with him had dived for cover as soon as Ellis had called out. Heggerty raised his head above a large boulder.

'Nice goin', Marshal,' Heggerty replied. 'We all had you figured as hidin' out there somewhere.'

'The thing is, I've got the girl now,' responded Ellis. 'I'll do a deal with you. I take her out of here, right now and you and the others are free to go where you will.'

'What about Paxton?' asked Heggerty.

'Him too,' Ellis agreed, rather reluctantly.

'Sounds too easy,' said Heggerty. 'What's the catch?'

'No catch,' promised Ellis. 'All I want is to

get the girl back where she belongs unharmed.'

'You're outgunned,' another voice pointed out which Ellis recognized as being Sam Paxton. 'Why the hell should we listen to you. There's nobody out here to know what happened if we do kill you.'

'You'll hang,' replied Ellis. 'I'll see to that, I promise you even if it takes years. As for the rest of you, I heard every word you said while you were sittin' by the fire. I was in a cellar right under your feet. As I see it, the only one among you who is wanted for murder is Paxton, I'll forget I ever heard anythin' about that saddletramp you say you killed, Heggerty. None of you are big enough for me to worry too much over but you'd be well advised to keep out of my territory in future.'

'Kelly an' Harper?' asked Heggerty.

'In the cellar, both still alive,' assured Ellis.

'No tricks?' said Heggerty again. 'You ride straight out of here tonight?'

'Agreed,' said Ellis.

'I can't decide for the others,' said Heggerty. 'I need to talk with them, includin' Kelly an' Harper.'

'They stay where they are,' replied Ellis. 'I don't think they'll disagree with what you decide.'

'I'll think about it, give me ten minutes.'

'There's nothin' to think about as far as I'm concerned,' growled Paxton. 'I say we blast him to hell.'

'This ain't your decision,' grated Heggerty. 'OK, Marshal, ten minutes.'

Almost exactly ten minutes later, as promised, Heggerty's voice echoed around. 'You got yourself a deal, Marshal, you're free to leave right now.'

'We need horses,' said Ellis.

'I thought of that,' laughed Heggerty. 'Seth an' John are saddlin' two up right now, yours an' the one the girl came in with.'

In confirmation two horses were led to the front of the store and the man quickly disappeared. Ellis looked at Mary and nodded slightly.

'I'm ready,' she confirmed.

Warily, Ellis led the way out of the store and helped Mary on to her horse. He looked round and could see the three outlaws, Heggerty, O'Rourke and Chaplin standing alongside the bunkhouse, each with rifles across their chest ready for action.

'Where's Paxton?' asked Ellis.

'Right here!' snarled Paxton, coming from behind the main building, hand raised, legs spread apart. 'Die, Marshal...'

There seemed to be a volley of shots and certainly Ellis could never have counted them as echoes rebounded all around. Sam Paxton stared wide-eyed and open-mouthed for a moment before blood choked in his throat and trickled from his mouth and he slumped to the ground.

'I guess you can have that one on us,' said Heggerty, lowering his rifle. 'Does that count as murder, Marshal?'

'Not in my book,' said Ellis, studying the body. 'I guess I'm goin' to need another horse...'

Marshal Ellis Stack grinned as he stepped forward to kiss the bride. As best man at the wedding of Sheriff Hal Gibson and Mary Howard he at least had that prerogative.

'You just look after him,' he said to her, 'and you make sure you treat her right,' he added, looking at Hal. 'Just remember, you're the sheriff now, don't let Mrs O'Hara order you about.'

'She won't,' assured Hal. 'I hear she's thinkin' of leavin' town anyhow.'

Hal stepped forward and shook the hands of two man-mountains, both of whom had had some of their hair cut for the occasion.

'Last time we saw a weddin' was back up in Canada. Indian weddin' that was...'

Ellis laughed and guided both bride and groom away from the two trappers. 'I reckon they've already spent most of their two hundred. Now, I have to get back. You still have a few things to learn. If there's any way I can help, you just send me a wire.'

'I hear you know a thing or two about women,' grinned Hal. 'I was wonderin' if you could give me a few tips on...'

'Hal Gibson!' scolded Mary. 'If you want to know anythin' about women you just make sure you ask me...'

This Large Print Book for the partially sighted, who cannot read normal print, is published under the auspices of
THE ULVERSCROFT FOUNDATION

THE ULVERSCROFT FOUNDATION

... we hope that you have enjoyed this Large Print Book. Please think for a moment about those people who have worse eyesight problems than you ... and are unable to even read or enjoy Large Print, without great difficulty.

You can help them by sending a donation, large or small to:

**The Ulverscroft Foundation,
1, The Green, Bradgate Road,
Anstey, Leicestershire, LE7 7FU,
England.**
or request a copy of our brochure for more details.

The Foundation will use all your help to assist those people who are handicapped by various sight problems and need special attention.

Thank you very much for your help.